THE MIDNIGHT LIBRARY

—

LIAR

DAMIEN GRAVES

SCHOLASTIC INC.

New York Toronto London Auckland Sydney
Mexico City New Delhi Hong Kong Buenos Aires

SPECIAL THANKS TO
TINA BARRETT

—

ISBN-13: 978-0-439-89392-3
ISBN-10: 0-439-89392-5

Series created by Working Partners Ltd.
Text copyright © 2006 by Working Partners Ltd.
Interior illustrations copyright © 2006 by David McDougall

12 11 10 9 8 7 6 5 4 3 2   7 8 9 10 11 12/0

Printed in the U.S.A.
First printing, May 2007

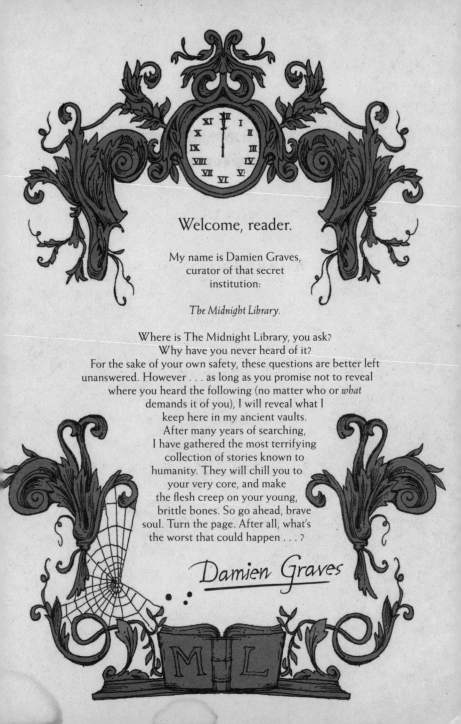

Welcome, reader.

My name is Damien Graves,
curator of that secret
institution:

The Midnight Library.

Where is The Midnight Library, you ask?
Why have you never heard of it?
For the sake of your own safety, these questions are better left
unanswered. However . . . as long as you promise not to reveal
where you heard the following (no matter who or *what*
demands it of you), I will reveal what I
keep here in my ancient vaults.
After many years of searching,
I have gathered the most terrifying
collection of stories known to
humanity. They will chill you to
your very core, and make
the flesh creep on your young,
brittle bones. So go ahead, brave
soul. Turn the page. After all, what's
the worst that could happen . . . ?

Damien Graves

LOOKING FOR DAYLIGHT? KEEP DREAMING.

THE MIDNIGHT LIBRARY CONTINUES....

—

VOICES

BLOOD AND SAND

END GAME

THE CAT LADY

LIAR

SHUT YOUR MOUTH

I CAN SEE YOU

THE
MIDNIGHT LIBRARY:
VOLUME V

Stories by Tina Barrett

—

CONTENTS

LIAR

Lauren Wolfe pressed her forehead against the glass of the bus window. It was cold and hard against her skin, and she felt every bump and jolt of the short trip home from school. She was seated alone as usual, the rest of her classmates gathered in groups in the back of the bus, chatting and laughing easily together. She was thirteen today, and not a single person had wished her "Happy Birthday."

Through the rain-spattered pane, she watched a young mom push a stroller along the main road. Lauren was suddenly grateful for her warm seat inside the bus as the stream of cars and buses sailed straight past the woman and the baby, soaking them with spray. Lauren pulled her head away in shock as the woman crossed in front of them without looking, shoving herself and the stroller into the street. The cars skidded to a shuddering halt, and Lauren cried out in alarm as the bus driver slammed on his brakes, throwing everyone perilously forward in their seats.

"Take it easy, driver!" yelled a boy from the last row of seats.

Lauren managed to steady herself by grabbing the steel rail in back of the driver's seat. She could hear other passengers complaining behind her as they struggled to sit up straight.

"Who gave you a driver's license?" someone shouted at the driver.

"Probably didn't have driver's licenses when he was young," teased someone else. "Only horses."

Everyone laughed, including Lauren. She looked around for someone to share the joke with but found no one. *Friends will come*, she told herself with a sigh. *You've only been at this school for two weeks. Things will be different here, you'll see.*

As the driver pulled away again, she pressed her head against the window once more just to feel the coldness of the glass beneath her skin and to reassure herself that she really did exist.

The bus rattled on, its doors spitting out passengers along the route with a snakelike hiss. Behind Lauren, noisy chatter turned to squeals and shrieks, and Lauren strained to hear why her classmates were laughing. Lauren hated the fact that she was so shy. She felt tears prick her eyes — and immediately clawed them back. She had always felt crippled by her shyness. At her last school, it had gripped her so tightly that Lauren had eventually given up trying to make friends, settling instead for becoming wallpaper. Wallpaper, she realized, just hung in the background, largely unnoticed by anyone. It was a lonely existence, but she reasoned that it was better than being laughed at.

For the next two stops, Lauren eavesdropped silently from behind the headrest. She listened to a bunch of girls from her class who were sitting near the back and chatting eagerly about clothes and shopping. She had a fair idea of the names of most of these girls, especially the one who was talking the most —

her name was Chantelle, and she was *popular*. She had effortless-looking dark hair and startling blue eyes. And she always seemed to buy the coolest clothes and accessories.

"Limited-edition hoop earrings, with rhinestones around the rim . . . forty percent off at the mall," said Chantelle. Lauren watched the others huddle around and admire the new accessories with loud *oohs* and *aahs*.

She felt her own earlobes; they were bare. She never wore earrings — or any jewelry for that matter. Fashion wasn't something Lauren knew that much about. She felt her cheeks burn with jealousy. She wondered what it felt like to be confident, to be the center of attention, and to have all your classmates surrounding you, giving you admiring glances and compliments. She bet it felt good.

And then it happened. Lauren had been so lost in her own thoughts that she hadn't noticed somebody sit down next to her. But this "somebody" wasn't just anybody. It was a boy. In fact, he looked like he could star in his own music video on MTV.

4

The boy smiled at her — a wide, friendly kind of smile. "Aren't you the new girl? Laura, right?"

He had a pair of huge chocolate-brown eyes and floppy dark curls. Lauren tried to stop staring like an idiot and concentrate on what he was saying.

She struggled to reply. "I . . . I'm . . . erm . . . I mean . . . hi." She kicked herself for sounding like a complete dork. She'd wanted to say *Hi! Actually, my name's Lauren, not Laura, but it's really nice to meet you.* But instead, she just found herself smiling like a lunatic.

"Well, anyway, my name's Marcus Hodges."

Lauren watched as Marcus made his way back down the aisle. She'd give anything to have a boyfriend like that!

For a moment, Lauren allowed herself to consider it, and her heart fluttered. Well, hadn't he sat next to her? And he knew her name, too! OK, so he had called her "Laura" instead of "Lauren" — but it was a start. At least he had noticed her. Her cheeks flushed hot at the thought and a grin spread across her face. Perhaps things *would* be different here after all. Her birthday was beginning to look up.

Lauren glanced around the edge of her seat but immediately wished she hadn't. Marcus was standing right beside Chantelle, and they were so close the tips of their noses almost touched. Chantelle was giggling and smiling while he tied a scarf around her neck, passing a hand over her new round earrings.

Lauren burned with embarrassment. How *stupid* she was to think that a boy like Marcus would ever be interested in someone like *her*. She reached for her schoolbag as the bus drew close to her stop. Standing at the doors, she gave Marcus and Chantelle a final glance. They were still standing close, wrapped up in their own little world. As Lauren stepped off the bus, she was suddenly angry. For the first time since she could remember, she was fed up with being wallpaper.

I am not going to be invisible anymore! she vowed as she marched up the street toward home.

As she walked home in the rain, Lauren knew that it was *definitely* a chocolate day. Chocolate was always a friend — even if none of her classmates were. Lauren headed for the convenience store on the corner of her street. Pushing open the door, she searched for change in her purse.

Inside, row upon row of bright colored wrappers stretched out enticingly before her, and Lauren studied them all in search of the one she wanted. Eventually, she picked a large milk chocolate bar.

"That's a lot of chocolate for a tiny girl," joked the man behind the counter, pointing at her skinny frame.

Lauren handed over the money. "I'm treating myself," she said, forcing a smile. "It's my birthday."

She ripped open the wrapper and broke off a chunk. Except for the incident with Marcus on the bus, Lauren realized that nobody had spoken to her all day. *Maybe this is how every birthday will be*, she thought miserably as she bit into the chocolate.

"Ooh, your face could spoil milk," laughed the man. "One would never guess you're celebrating today."

"I'm sorry, what?" said Lauren, not understanding what the man meant.

"Aren't you throwing a party?" He was all smiles.

The chocolate stuck in Lauren's throat. She had nothing like that planned. In fact, she didn't even know if her parents would be there when she got home. They were always working late.

"You *are* having a party, aren't you?" the man asked, when Lauren didn't reply.

"Me? Oh, yes, of course I am." She forced a smile.

The man put a large pile of glossy-looking magazines in a plastic shopping bag and handed them to Lauren. "Well, here's a little gift from me, anyway. They're only back issues, but you can share them with all your friends."

Lauren smiled. She was really touched by the man's kindness. However, the fact that only a stranger had bothered to wish her a happy birthday today just made matters worse. She felt the muscles in her cheeks twitch and she knew that was the first sign of tears.

"Thanks for these," she said quietly. "I think I'll take another chocolate bar before I go."

As she had suspected, the house was empty when Lauren returned, but she didn't actually mind as much as she thought she would. She walked into the kitchen and found a pile of cards on the table. She picked up the envelopes, recognizing the handwriting on each one — all cousins and aunts and uncles. It was nice, but not as nice as if she had gotten some cards from her friends. Then Lauren heard the front door open.

"Hello? Birthday girl!" her father called out.

"Dad!" Lauren responded, running into the hallway and giving her dad a big hug.

"I wanted to get back early for your birthday, but the traffic was murder. Sorry about that."

"That's fine," Lauren said, not letting her dad go.

"You OK, darling?" he said, concern clouding his features.

"I'm all right now, Dad — it's just nice to see you," Lauren replied.

"Come and see what your mom and I got you!"

Her face split into a grin. This was more like it!

"Thirteen today," he said, planting a kiss on top of her head. "You'll be off to college in no time."

"I'll be able to drive a car first!" she laughed.

Lauren covered her eyes with her hands, and her dad led her down the hall toward the front room.

The front door slammed again. "Only me," called

her mother. "The traffic's a nightmare tonight. Have you started without me? No peeping yet," she teased. "Not till we tell you to."

Lauren heard the sound of plastic bags rustling and boxes opening. She could barely contain her excitement. "Hurry up," she urged.

"OK, OK," said her dad, removing her hands from her eyes. "You can open them now."

There in front of her on the dining-room table was a brand-new computer.

Lauren gasped in delight. "Is that for me?"

"Yes, it is," said her mother. "You can put it in your room."

"It's got a flat screen, a remote-controlled mouse, and a broadband Internet connection," said her dad, ever the computer nut.

"It's the best present ever," Lauren said happily. "Can we set it up?"

"First things first," said her mother. "I picked up some Chinese food for dinner — your favorite!"

Lauren beamed. It was turning out to be quite a good birthday after all — until the conversation at the dinner table turned to school.

"Good day?" her mother asked over a shrimp roll.

"Great," Lauren lied.

"You could have invited a friend over if you'd wanted to," her mother ventured.

"I know," said Lauren, not looking up from her plate. She felt her face go red. How could she explain she didn't actually have any friends to invite over? Her father came to the rescue.

"Darling, this *is* Lauren we're talking about," he said, giving her a wink. "She's far too busy with school-work for that kind of thing. In fact," Dad began in his changing-the-subject voice, "I was talking to a colleague at work today. He's got a daughter in Lauren's class. I think she's called Chanteuse or Canterelle or something. . . ."

"Chantelle," corrected Lauren.

"That's right! Well, apparently he's got his hands full with her. She's always on the Internet, exchanging messages with friends. Her grades are plummeting, and she never gets any schoolwork done."

"You won't do that, will you, Lauren?" her mom said, wondering if Lauren's gift had been a bad idea.

"I didn't mean that Lauren —" her dad began.

"Of course I won't, Mom," Lauren replied, cutting her father off mid-sentence. Lauren's favorite noodles suddenly tasted like straw. If her father had meant to cheer her up, he had failed miserably. She tried to eat the rest of her dinner, but her appetite had disappeared.

"Can we set up my computer now, Dad?" she asked, anxious to leave the table and the conversation.

Lauren watched her dad fire a look of concern at her mom. "I'll be with you in a couple of minutes, sweetheart. Why don't you go and watch some TV?"

Lauren excused herself and slumped down on the sofa. She could feel a tiny flame of desire ignite inside her.

She wanted to be one of the girls at the center of the chat in a chat room.

She wanted to know about music and clothes.

As Lauren let the TV program wash over her, she realized she felt sick to death of knowing about algebra and geometry and boring stuff that never seemed to help her, ever.

A little while later, Lauren was sitting at the desk in her bedroom, the computer connected and ready to boot up. She gave her dad a kiss. "Thanks. I love my present," she said. "It's magnificent."

"If you need any help," he said, disappearing around the bedroom door, "just give me a shout." Before he left, he reached inside his jacket and got out his credit card. "Get yourself some books with this, if you like. Happy birthday, hon."

"Thanks, Dad!" Lauren replied.

Lauren flicked the switch and the monitor burst to life. She grinned in anticipation. A computer — she'd been begging her parents for over a year now! Quickly, she connected to the Internet and then sat back. *Where should I go first?* Without really thinking, she reached for the keyboard and typed "rock music" into the search engine.

Thousands of listings flashed up in front of her, and she suddenly felt swamped. What was the name of the band that she had heard the girls talking about that day at school? She wanted to buy some music, not some more books. Her hand froze over the mouse. The trouble was that Lauren wasn't absolutely sure what the band was called. What if she bought the wrong CDs?

Suddenly, Lauren had an idea. The magazines that the man in the shop had given her! There *had* to be some information in those that could help her out. And sure enough, after only a moment's searching, she found a feature called "In and Out: What's Hot and What's Not! A Need-to-Know Guide."

Lauren studied it intently. The IN column featured a list of all the things currently in fashion while the OUT column contained all the things going out of fashion.

Apparently, rhinestone hoop earrings were currently out of fashion. Lauren couldn't resist smiling at that piece of information.

Underneath the IN heading she read that ballerina shoes, denim skirts, and long scarves were the *must-have* clothes items at the moment. Red lipstick was out while pink lip gloss was in. At last, she came to the part she was looking for, the music section. According to *Teen Power* and confirmed by *Girl Spirit*, Scum was on the way out and the Chinchillas were all the rage, mainly because of their super-cool lead singer, Luke Skyler.

Lauren picked up her dad's credit card. The Chinchillas' album stared enticingly at her from the screen. Before she could change her mind, Lauren was clicking the CD into her shopping cart and, when the prompt came up, she began typing the number of the credit card into the secure server.

The payment screen came up immediately. *"Thank you for shopping. Your purchase will be shipped immediately. Please click here to continue shopping."*

Now that her dad's credit card details were stored on the Web site, Lauren found herself ordering two more CDs recommended in one of the magazines. After signing off, she became completely absorbed by the Hollywood gossip and beauty articles. There was a section entirely dedicated to the best online communities. Apparently, many of her classmates were logging on to them in the school library. As a result, the sites had become banned during school hours. Lauren had heard some of the kids from her class discussing a particular site called the Outer Zone. Apparently, it had a forum where teens discussed all of the cool stuff happening in their area, so it was mostly visited by users from her school and the neighboring town's schools.

Lauren's mind wandered. She wondered if Marcus Hodges chatted on the Outer Zone. Suddenly, she was seized by a sudden urge to go online and find out. A surge of excitement rushed through her as she considered what she would do if Marcus really *did* use the site. Perhaps she could get to know him through the forum. At least online, her tongue wouldn't tie itself up in knots.

The thought energized her. Before she could stop herself, she had typed the address into her browser. Her finger hovered nervously above the mouse button. She was only a click away when she heard her father's voice from the foot of the stairs. "Have you found anything you like, Lauren?"

Lauren immediately turned off the monitor. "Er . . . yes, thanks, Dad!" she called down.

She shut down her new PC and got changed for bed — except she wasn't tired at all. She was thinking hard. *If I'm going to stop being invisible*, she thought, *then I'll make sure I'm noticed for all the right reasons*. She got into bed with a pile of the magazines next to her. When she visited the Outer Zone, Lauren was determined to be prepared.

—

Over the next week, Lauren studied the magazines and Web sites for the latest music and fashion trends. She received her new CDs in the mail, and actually enjoyed them a lot. She was beginning to feel confident about her knowledge and tastes. When she wasn't listening to music, she was listening to her classmates in the school cafeteria or on the bus ride home. In an effort to familiarize herself with the latest gossip, Lauren had started taking a seat halfway down the bus instead of her usual place in the front row. It was the perfect setup for her to tune in to what was going on.

After a few days, Lauren made up her mind. Tonight would be the night she'd take the bull by the horns and venture into the Outer Zone.

When she'd finished supper, Lauren went to her bedroom and booted up her computer. As she waited nervously for it to load, she put on one of her new CDs and turned up the volume. Within seconds, screaming guitar riffs filled her bedroom, and suddenly, the Outer Zone was on her screen. Bright neon colors glared out at her from a purple background. Lauren blinked her eyes, trying to find her bearings on the page. At the top of the screen, a blinking banner welcomed her. *The Outer Zone*, it read. *THE Place to Be.*

Underneath, images of perfect-looking teenagers all dressed in the latest fashions seemed to be chatting and laughing together. *Welcome to the coolest community on the Web*, read a tagline underneath. *Today's hot topics are: Celebrity Scoop, Music Buzz, Chitchat, Fashion and Beauty.*

Just then, she noticed a link at the top of the page. *Welcome, Newbie*, it read. *Want to sign in as a guest and visit your local forum? Click here to begin!*

It was just what she needed. She clicked the link gratefully.

Thank you, Guest, flashed the reply. *You are now logged in and can leave messages on any of the Outer Zone's boards.*

The screen changed and the Music Buzz Message Board welcomed her. To Lauren's frustration, she found she had even more choices to make. The banner read, *Threads in Music Buzz*, and below that was another list.

This is so complicated, she said to herself. She glided the cursor over the various categories for discussion: *Pop, Country, Rap, Garage Rock*. Lauren knew nothing about any of it, but just as she was going to go to another topic, she saw a discussion topic called *The Rise of the Chinchillas.*

Finally, a band I know something about. She smiled to herself.

A long list of messages about the Chinchillas scrolled down the screen with a REPLY button beside each one in case anybody had a comment or reply.

Luke Skyler of the Chinchillas is so creative! read one of the messages.

Has anybody met him? wrote someone called ChanD. Lauren felt a jolt of worry shoot through her entire body. Could that be Chantelle? After all, her last name was Dawson.

Next, Lauren scanned the long list of posts in search of a screen name that might have belonged to Marcus. Lauren felt a little dejected. There didn't seem to be any screen names resembling Marcus's name. Eventually, she found a link revealing which members were currently logged on to the forum. She recognized some of the screen names such as ChanD for Chantelle Dawson and JoC for Chantelle's best friend, Josie Culver. Yet there was nobody online who seemed like Marcus.

She was all set to sign out when curiosity got the

better of her. She found herself clicking the REPLY button to Chantelle's question about Luke Skyler, lead singer of the Chinchillas.

It wouldn't hurt to reply, Lauren thought. *After all, I'm signed in as "Guest." Nobody knows who I am.* She began to type.

I haven't actually met Luke Skyler, she began, *but I do know a ton of stuff about him.*

With a deep breath, Lauren clicked on a button reading POST TO MESSAGE BOARD.

Immediately, she saw her message flash up alongside the screen name "Guest." She was breathless with excitement. She'd done it! She wondered if Chantelle would even bother to answer, but almost immediately, a reply came back.

Hi, Guest, Chantelle had written. *Tell me everything.*

Lauren grinned, immediately pleased she had taken the risk. It was a good thing she'd read Luke Skyler's profile in *Now* magazine this morning.

Well — I know he's a Gemini and that his birthday's June 12. His fave food is French fries and he was born in Amsterdam.

She posted the message and waited for a reply. It didn't take long. She definitely had Chantelle's attention now.

Cool, came the reply. *I luv fries, too. He's such a babe. We have soooo much in common. What else do you know? BTW, who are you, Guest?*

The last question hit Lauren like a thunderbolt. She was suddenly stumped. Should she reveal herself yet?

Panicking slightly, she took a moment to compose her answer. *It doesn't matter who I am*, Lauren wrote back. *I'm a massive Chinchillas fan, just like you.* She tried to change the subject. *Their new album is terrific, especially the song called "You're Gone." It's got a brilliant instrumental part at the end where the violins go really crazy.*

But as soon as she'd posted the message she knew she'd made a mistake. Back came the reply within seconds: *Violins? Are U crazy?*

Lauren's palms were drenched with sweat. Nobody at her school discussed classical instruments! They talked about guitar riffs, cool lead singers, and earrings. She was out of her depth and drowning fast. She had to fix her mistake.

Only joking, she typed. *Did you know Luke Skyler's favorite color is purple?*

Everybody knows that, came back the response from

ChanD. Then another one in quick succession. *Tell us who you are, "Guest." We don't appreciate uninvited visitors on our board — especially losers who lie to fit in. Come on — who are you?*

Lauren was now really worried. She made a snap decision, and began to type. *I think that you might know me from the bus to school. My name's Lauren.*

But it was too late. A nasty reply appeared — for anybody to read.

Oh, I totally know who U R! it read. *U R that geek girl who hides behind the seats spying on everyone. Only a dork like U would obsess over violins. Nice try by pretending to like the Chinchillas, though — LOL!*

Lauren's cheeks burned with shame as she watched other replies flashing up thick and fast.

Laurentheloser! read another message from ChanD.

Y don't U get a life? JoC's posting said.

Get lost, loooooooser!!!!!! the final message from ChanD said.

"No!" she shouted to herself in frustration. Lauren sank back into her chair, tears prickling her eyes. Why did this have to happen? Her heart sank. She closed the screen and signed off. Those girls would never be her friends now. The only comfort Lauren felt was, as far as she could tell, Marcus hadn't been online tonight to see her humiliated.

With any luck, he would never find out.

But Lauren was wrong. When she arrived at school the next morning, people began to point at her and laugh. It seemed that Chantelle had told everyone.

"Oh, look," Chantelle said as Lauren took her place in homeroom. "Here comes the Guest! Too bad she's an unwelcome one!"

Everybody laughed, including Marcus, and Lauren felt just as if she had been thumped in the chest. Why couldn't she have just stuck to being anonymous? She was the center of attention now, but not for any of the reasons she'd wanted.

"What did you expect, Laura?" Marcus said. "You should have just been yourself, instead of trying to hide. That would have been enough."

Lauren felt more mixed up and confused than ever as she watched him walk away. Be herself? Lauren hadn't even thought of that. Well, maybe, just maybe, it was worth a try!

—

That night, inspired by Marcus's words, Lauren decided to make another effort. She signed on once more to the Outer Zone. This time she decided to make it clear who she was. She took the screen name "UnwantedGuest." Lauren was determined to do exactly as Marcus said. She would talk to the others without hiding.

She found her classmates posting in the local Chitchat area and decided to start a new thread.

Hi, Guys, she wrote. *It's the unwanted guest! Sorry about last night. Does anybody want to chat?*

Lauren saw her message flash up on the screen and waited.

Five minutes passed.

Then ten. Nobody replied.

Perhaps they're all having their dinner, Lauren thought hopefully. She clicked on the link showing current members still active in the Outer Zone, and her hopes sank. They were all still online. They just weren't posting on Lauren's thread.

Lauren gave it a final shot.

Realize you must all be annoyed about last night, but I'm really sorry. Can we chat? she typed, her fingers trembling slightly.

Fifteen more minutes passed with no replies.

Bitterness and anger welled up inside her. What was it Marcus had said? She should be herself, and that would be enough. Well, tonight was proving otherwise.

Being herself was *not* enough.

Chantelle and the others clearly didn't want to know Lauren, whether she was the "Guest" or herself. She logged off, feeling miserable. She slammed the mouse down on the desk and shut off her computer. Trying to make herself feel better, she put on the Chinchillas, but as the music began, she hated every word of Luke Skyler's lyrics and jabbed the STOP button with her finger.

As she sat there, dejected, Lauren saw one of the magazines open nearby, and a beautiful model was staring up at her from the pages. "If only I was you," she told the girl on the page. "Then everyone would want to know me."

Lauren sat bolt upright. As soon as the words had left her mouth, an idea came into her head. She immediately knew what to do.

She sat down once more in front of her computer and waited impatiently for it to boot up. Once online, she headed straight for the Outer Zone. Clicking open the registration page, Lauren feverishly edited her member profile. It was so obvious! Marcus had told Lauren to try being herself — but he had been wrong. All her life she had been herself and it had never been good enough. She began to search for her classmates on Chitchat.

If people didn't like Lauren for who she was, then the answer was to become someone *completely different*.

As she typed, a broad grin spread across Lauren's face. This was going to be fun.

Hi, guys, my name's Jennifer, it read. *And I've just met Luke Skyler from the Chinchillas. Anybody wanna hear about it?*

Lauren was amazed how quickly the time flew by. So many people wanted to chat with "Jennifer" that she didn't shut down her computer until nearly midnight.

Chantelle had been the first to reply, demanding all the gossip about Jennifer's encounter with Luke Skyler. Lauren had hesitated slightly before typing in her first reply. She knew that everything she typed in as Jennifer would have to be a lie, and Lauren didn't like lying. *But Jennifer's not real, so what's the problem?* she said to herself, and began to type.

I do a little modeling and bumped into the Chinchillas at one of my photo shoots. Luke Skyler was an absolute babe, even better than he looks in his photos. He was insanely nice, too, not stuck-up or anything. He even gave me a kiss and signed my T-shirt because I didn't have any paper.

Lauren posted the message. As it flashed up on the screen, she reread it. It was such a fantastic lie that she couldn't believe anybody would buy it. But to her amazement — and intense satisfaction — they did.

In fact, she had loads of replies, not just from Chantelle, but from Josie, plus at least a dozen other people from her school that she could recognize from their screen names. She read their comments with amazement.

U lucky girl!

Do u think u could help me meet him?

Are u really a model?

How did you get to be a model?

Which designers do U model for?

Lauren laughed at the last one. She hadn't imagined anyone would *really* believe Jennifer was a model. She thumbed through her magazines to see if she could find suitable inspiration for her reply.

I was spotted in the street by a top agency. I have modeled for all the best designers — from Calvin Klein to plenty of others. But modeling is very boring. When I graduate, I want to go to art school. But I am also captain of my school hockey team and an Olympic coach has suggested I try out for the squad when I turn sixteen. It's a tough decision. What would u do?

As Lauren posted, she realized that she had a wide smile on her face. This was as happy as she'd felt in a long time. She was in control, and she was the center of attention. And, more important, everyone —

including Chantelle and Josie — seemed to think that she was cool.

But then she reread her last post. It seemed ridiculous to her — over-the-top and flimsy. Surely someone would challenge her? For a nervous minute, she waited for the screen to refresh itself.

I would be a model, answered JoC.

Most definitely, replied ChanD. *Be a model!*

For the next few days when she got home from school, Lauren pretended that she was going directly upstairs to do her homework, but she was actually creating the world that Jennifer lived in. She wanted to make sure that every part of her imaginary life was covered.

By day, Lauren was still the quiet and mostly ignored girl at school, but at night, she became Jennifer, a super-cool model with beautiful, long blonde hair. When she was Jennifer, Lauren felt glamorous and envied.

Then, one night, a new member arrived. And the name stopped Lauren's heart for a second. She was sure it was Marcus Hodges.

Hi, Jen, MarcH wrote.

Lauren took a deep breath. *Hi there, MarcH!* she replied.

They began to talk about a new film that she hadn't seen, but she'd read a few reviews of it online.

So glad I'm not the only film geek! MarcH replied.

Sequels r usually worthless, Lauren wrote, *but this one was saved by the great acting.*

You are TOTALLY right! MarcH replied.

Lauren couldn't believe how well she and Marcus were hitting it off! *Well,* she reminded herself, *it's Marcus and Jennifer that are getting along this well.*

The next day, Lauren was in the cafeteria eating her sandwich when Marcus, Chantelle, and Josie sat down at the table next to hers.

The talk turned to movies. Lauren listened in as Marcus told the others about the film that she and he had talked about the night before.

"The effects were incredible," he was telling the others. "You should go and see it."

Aidan, a friend of Marcus's, joined them at the table. "What's going on? What are you talking about,

Marcus?" he said, grabbing a doughnut off Josie's tray and stuffing it into his mouth.

"That film I went to see, remember?" Marcus replied.

"But it's rated R. How did you get in?" Josie asked.

"I have my ways," Marcus said with a grin.

"Well, you do look much older than us, Marcus," said Chantelle, smiling coyly.

Lauren hated the way that Chantelle pandered to Marcus. But to Lauren's surprise, Marcus barely reacted. "Thanks, Chan, but as I was saying, the effects were incredible. In one of the scenes, the main character tumbles right off a cliff still clinging to the back of his horse and amazingly —"

"— they land at the bottom, completely untouched, and then ride off into battle and save the castle," Lauren finished.

Everyone at Marcus's table stopped and turned around to see who had just spoken. She was so caught up listening to the conversation, Lauren had inadvertently finished the sentence.

"That's right!" Marcus said. "That's exactly right. And the main guy even —"

"— did his own stunts, apparently," Lauren finished. She could feel Marcus watching her, and her cheeks began to burn.

Chantelle flashed her an angry look. "How did you know that?"

"She must have seen it, of course," answered Marcus. He turned to Lauren. "Am I right?"

Lauren nodded, unable to think of a better reply. But it was clear to her that Chantelle wasn't buying it.

"Liar!" she sneered at Lauren. "How could a little geek like you get into an R-rated movie? You don't even look old enough for a PG film!"

The comment stung Lauren, but instead of feeling like retreating into her shell, she felt something else — confidence. After all, Jennifer had told *much* bigger lies on the Outer Zone, but the other girls had been eager enough to swallow those. Clearly, Chantelle was only angry because Lauren — and not Jennifer — had commented on the film. If Jennifer were commenting, then there would have been no argument.

"Well, I did see the movie, as a matter of fact," Lauren replied, staring at Chantelle hotly. "My friend and I snuck in, and we watched it from the back row." She could feel Marcus's full attention on her, and it filled Lauren with confidence. "But we were caught by the usher halfway through so we didn't manage to see the end."

"Cool," said Marcus, grinning. "I can fill you in on the parts you missed if you like." He got up to join her at the table, but Chantelle grabbed his arm and dragged him back down.

"I wouldn't bother," she said. "It's all a bunch of lies. I've never seen her with any friends, *ever*."

"I'm telling the *truth!*" Lauren replied. She refused to let Chantelle ruin her moment in the spotlight.

Chantelle looked her straight in the eye. "All right then, if you're telling the truth, who is this mysterious friend of yours?"

Lauren felt sick with panic. What could she say? She saw Chantelle's eyes narrow, a glint of triumph in them.

"You wouldn't know her," Lauren began. "She doesn't go to this school."

"Yeah, right," laughed Chantelle. "That is *sooo* convenient."

"It's not convenient," replied Lauren in a steady

voice. "It's true. We've been best friends for years, but we see each other less often now because my family moved. Plus, she's usually away on a modeling job."

There was momentary silence as Chantelle glared suspiciously at Lauren.

"Give her a break, Chan," urged Marcus.

"I'll drop it as soon as she tells me the name of this friend," Chantelle persisted.

For a moment, Lauren toyed with the idea of walking away from it all and pretending that it never happened. But she couldn't. Looking around, she realized that she was now the center of attention in real life, not just online. This was too good to give up for someone like Chantelle.

"Jennifer," Lauren said without flinching. "My friend's name is Jennifer."

For the rest of break, Marcus shared chips with Lauren and explained all the details about the end of the film that she and Jennifer had apparently missed. Lauren was too excited to focus on what he was saying. Reveling in her victory over Chantelle, she happily enjoyed sitting with the coolest boy in the school. His full attention was on her!

When she returned home, Lauren felt like she was floating. Everything had gone right for her . . . with a little help from Jennifer.

That night, she visited the Outer Zone, signing in as Jennifer. It wasn't long before Marcus began posting messages on her thread.

Hi, Jen, he wrote. *Got a question for u. U know how you said you saw the film? Did u take a friend?*

Lauren smiled to herself. *Yes, I did,* she replied. *Why do u ask?*

Well, I was talking to a girl named Laura at school today. She said she snuck into the film with her friend Jennifer. I wondered if it was u, or am I barking up the wrong tree?

Lauren felt a tingle of irritation. *Her name is Lauren, actually,* she typed. *And yes, I did go with her. She's such a cool friend. We've known each other forever. My dad's a surgeon and Lauren's mom's a medical researcher. We met at a boring hospital charity event. Lauren was such a scream that she totally rescued me from a long day in Dullsville, and we've been best friends ever since. UR so lucky she goes to your school. U should really get to know her.*

"Hopefully, he'll want to talk to Lauren — I mean, me — now," Lauren said aloud. But to her dismay, Marcus couldn't take his mind off of Jennifer.

His reply came back in an instant. *Actually . . . I'd rather get to know you, Jennifer. Y don't you send me your e-mail address so we can talk off the forum and get to know each other better?*

Lauren pushed away from the desk. Although she'd created a really great character, she hadn't bargained on *this* happening. Changing her screen name to "Jennifer" had been simple enough, but Lauren knew that she couldn't possibly give her own e-mail address to Marcus. He'd figure out everything in a flash and never speak to her again.

Marcus posted her again. *Come on, Jen! What's taking so long?*

In panic, Lauren typed in the first thing she could think of. *Got to go. CUL8er!*

She signed off, her heart beating fast. The lies were getting complicated now, and she didn't like having to trick someone as nice as Marcus. But on the other hand, Lauren had just had Marcus's undivided attention. Suddenly, the lies felt worth it.

The following morning, Lauren was just about to sit down in homeroom when she felt a gentle tap on her shoulder. She turned around and found herself face-to-face with Marcus. He looked a little nervous, and as he started to speak, Lauren thought that she heard him stammer slightly.

"Hi," he said. "I-er-I wondered if you've got a minute."

Lauren blushed. She noticed Chantelle scowling furiously at her, but it was obvious she was jealous that Marcus was giving Lauren so much close attention. *Thank you, Jennifer!* thought Lauren. *Perhaps the good word she'd put in for Lauren last night had paid off after all!* "Um, sure," she said, "what's up?"

Marcus took her arm and led her to a quiet corner of the classroom. "I wanted to give this to you," he said, passing her a scrap of paper.

Lauren looked down. She read the blue scrawl. It was Marcus's e-mail address. Lauren could hardly believe it. He'd considered all the nice things Jennifer had said about Lauren — and decided that he wanted to get to know Lauren better! She glowed with happiness.

"Is this . . . for me?" she asked, rereading the words on the paper.

Marcus nodded and smiled. "I thought you could pass it to your friend Jennifer, if you wouldn't mind. I tried to give it to her last night, but she had to rush off and didn't come back online. But you could give it to her, couldn't you? I know she's your best friend and everything."

Lauren suddenly felt sick. She nodded in silence, trying not to reveal her disappointment.

"Thanks, Lauren — that's awesome! I knew I could count on you. How soon can you give it to her?" Marcus said, beaming.

Well, at least he got my name right, Lauren thought. She pulled herself together. "Tonight," she replied, mustering the best smile that she could. "I'll give it to Jennifer tonight."

After supper, Lauren sat at her PC, head in hands. She didn't know what to do. All she had ever wanted was to get close to Marcus and fit in. But her plan was backfiring because all *he* wanted was to talk to Jennifer. She looked miserably at the scrap of paper on her desk.

She weighed the options. If she gave up the act now, nothing at school would have changed. Lauren shuddered at the thought of it. But if she kept up the lie and carried on pretending to be Jennifer, then she could continue putting in a good word for herself. Eventually, Marcus might come to see her in a new light and realize he preferred her to Jennifer. The whole series of events could still work out in her favor.

Feeling more positive, Lauren wasted no time in creating a brand new e-mail address for Jennifer to use.

Perfect, she said to herself.

Lauren saved Marcus's e-mail address in Jennifer's address book, and then she began to compose Jennifer's e-mail to him:

Hi, Marcus,
Got your address from Lauren today. Heard you might want mine. Here it is!
Jen

After the briefest time, there was one new message in Jennifer's in-box. Lauren smiled. Marcus must have been waiting for her to e-mail.

Hi, Jen,
Glad Lauren did what I asked her. What r u up to tonight?
R u doing homework or something more interesting?
Marcus

Lauren thought for a moment and then clicked on the REPLY button.

Me and Lauren r having a sleepover. I doubt I'll get any
sleep at all tonight because she is so hilarious! We'll proba-
bly still be giggling when the sun comes up tomorrow!
Jx

Lauren e-mailed Marcus all evening. "Jennifer" took every opportunity to vouch for how cool Lauren was. It was midnight when she eventually logged off. Feeling exhilarated, she flopped down into her bed, but then she remembered something awful: She hadn't done her homework! It was due to be handed in first period tomorrow. Normally the very thought of getting into trouble with a teacher would have terrified Lauren. But for some reason, it didn't tonight. She could only think about her correspondence with Marcus, until she eventually fell asleep.

Mr. Price's math class came all too soon for Lauren. She arrived five minutes late, her eyes dark and puffy from lack of sleep.

"So, Lauren. You've decided to grace us with your presence," said Mr. Price. "I trust you come bearing your algebra homework."

She hadn't and now she hated the thought of being in trouble. She could feel herself shrinking in front of the teacher and her classmates. But then something in her made her stop. *What would Jennifer do?* she asked herself. Lauren noticed Marcus smiling at her from the back of the classroom, and in that moment, she found exactly the right words to say. "I slept over at a friend's house last night, sir, and I'm afraid I left my math homework there. I only remembered at the bus stop, but when I went back to get it, her parents had already left for work. I couldn't get in the house. By that time, the bus had gone. That's why I'm late."

To Lauren's amazement, Mr. Price waved her away with a hand, saying, "Next time, don't be so careless. I'll expect it in tomorrow. No excuses."

"Yes, sir," Lauren replied, making her way to her desk. Even though she was tired, she suddenly felt fantastic! *Anyone who says that lying doesn't pay is simply a bad liar*, she thought, smiling.

She was still smiling about math class when she arrived at the school cafeteria. The place was packed, and it looked as if Lauren was out of luck finding an empty seat. But just then, Angie Johnson, one of the most popular girls in the school, got up from her seat and motioned toward Lauren.

Lauren turned around, thinking Angie must be waving at someone standing behind her. But there was nobody else there.

"Hey, Lauren," called Angie. "There's a seat over here."

Lauren walked over and sat down next to Angie. "Hi," she said.

"You're a friend of Jennifer's, aren't you?" Angie began. "Well, I'm having a party this weekend, and I thought you guys might like to come. She and I have shot a few messages back and forth on the Outer Zone and she seems pretty cool."

Lauren couldn't believe it. It was her first party invite and, to top it off, it was from Angie Johnson! She composed herself. "That sounds great, Angie. Let me speak to Jennifer and I'll get back to you."

Lauren dimly remembered chatting with someone named AnnG. She thought back to their discussion about modeling. She'd had no idea she'd been giving style advice to a girl as cool as Angie.

Chantelle arrived at their table. "I see you've got an unwelcome guest here, Angie," she said curtly.

"Do you mean Lauren?" Angie replied. "She's not unwelcome. In fact, I was just inviting her and Jennifer to my party this weekend."

Barely able to suppress a giggle, Lauren watched as Chantelle's face started to resemble a chewed gumball.

"That's right," Lauren added, looking Chantelle directly in the eye, "and I think *we* can come, as long as Jennifer hasn't got a modeling job or anything."

Wordlessly, Chantelle sat down and stared at her

lunch. Angie sat down next to Lauren. "Sorry about that," she began. "Now, tell me about Jen! It must be great having a model for a friend. You must get to share her clothes and everything."

"Oh, yeah," replied Lauren. "Jen's super-generous. Last week she gave me a pair of brand-new sandals. But then again, she's always been like that — ever since we met that first day of fourth grade."

"Wait a second," interrupted Chantelle. "Marcus told me that you two met at some sort of hospital charity event. Which one is it, Lauren?"

Lauren swallowed hard. *Was that really what she had told Marcus? That they had met at a charity event?* She thought back. It was true, she remembered telling him. Angie looked uncertain, her pretty features creased into a frown. Inside, Lauren kicked herself for making such a stupid mistake.

"Er . . . that's right," she said slowly, thinking on her feet, "and coincidentally, we both started at the same school the next day! That's why I got things mixed up. It was a while ago, after all."

To Lauren's relief, the lie seemed to have the desired effect: Chantelle didn't challenge her anymore, and

Angie seemed fine again. But it highlighted a problem. Lauren was beginning to tell so many lies about Jennifer, she was having difficulty remembering exactly what she'd said to whom. As she threw away her leftovers, she realized that she'd have to think of a way to fix the problem.

During her next study period, Lauren wrote everything down so that she wouldn't forget what she had said about Jennifer: height, eye color, hair color, likes, dislikes, friends, family, and hobbies. She put it all in a card folder and tucked the file into her schoolbag. Once it was finished, Lauren smiled. There was no way they'd find out the truth now.

That evening, Marcus was at soccer practice, so Lauren decided not to bother visiting the Outer Zone. She contented herself by listening to music and reading the new magazines she had bought on the way home from school.

But even though it had been another good day, Lauren slept poorly. She had a vivid dream about Jennifer. She was walking into Angie's party, and everyone was there — including Marcus. Soon, she was making her way through the crowd, and everyone was smiling and saying hello to her. And then she found herself dancing next to a blonde girl who looked like the model out of her magazine. *It's Jennifer*, she realized in shock. But this Jennifer certainly didn't seem to be the good friend that Lauren had created. *This* Jennifer turned around and stared her up and down, and Lauren could feel a wall of self-consciousness closing up around her. And then this Jennifer began to laugh . . . and as she kept laughing at her the sound grated on Lauren's ears.

"Please, stop it!" Lauren cried, trying to find a way out of the crowd, but failing because the party was packed. She could see Marcus nearby, but he was ignoring her — and seemed to be staring at Jennifer.

Then Jennifer began taunting her. "You'll get caught," she said mockingly. "You know it can't last."

Lauren tried desperately to dance away from Jennifer, but she couldn't get through the crowd. Suddenly, Jennifer lunged out and grabbed Lauren's arm tightly enough to bruise the skin. Lauren shouted at her to stop. But Jennifer seemed to find this funny, throwing back her head and laughing as the grip on Lauren's arm grew tighter and tighter.

She awoke with a jolt and turned on the bedside lamp. The dream was so real and terrifying, she felt she needed to look at her wrist. But there were no marks. Nothing. Lauren's heart still thumped in her chest. She looked at the alarm clock: It said 3:12. Leaving on the light, Lauren rolled over and tried not to think about Jennifer.

Lauren arrived at school tired and flustered. The late nights were taking a toll on her now. Last night's bad dream hadn't helped much, either, and Lauren was still trying to cope with it when she got to class. By lunchtime, her head was throbbing. She was beginning to feel short-tempered. All anybody wanted to discuss was Jennifer.

"Will Jennifer be modeling at New York Fashion Week?" asked Angie.

Or, from the boys: "Has Jennifer got a date for Angie's party?"

Even though it had been Lauren who had created

Jennifer, she was getting tired of the whole performance. She almost wished to be anonymous again so she could get a little peace and quiet.

As she walked out toward the playground, she heard footsteps from behind her. It was Josie, Chantelle's friend who'd been mean to her when she first posted on the Web site.

"Hi, Lauren," said Josie, "I've been looking for you everywhere! Anyway, I wanted to tell you that I met your friend Jennifer in town on Saturday. Isn't that great?"

Lauren felt as though her heart had stopped. "Are you sure?" she replied.

"Oh, yeah," continued Josie. "I was buying some new jeans when I noticed her standing on line at the cash register. Of course, I knew it was Jennifer right away. Long blonde hair, perfect skin, and those long legs — well, no wonder she's a model!"

Lauren tried to see whether Josie had been somehow put up to this. Was she trying to trick her? Josie appeared to be telling the truth. *But it didn't make sense.* There was no way she could have met Jennifer, because Jennifer didn't exist.

"Did you speak to her?" Lauren asked, recovering

enough to think a little more clearly. "Did she actually tell you who she was?"

Josie nodded. "Oh, yes. I asked, and she told me she was named Jennifer. She was really nice about it."

"And what happened next?"

"Well," Josie continued, "it was her turn to pay for her stuff, so we didn't really have any time to chat. When I came back, she was gone. Probably due at another modeling job or something . . ."

That night, Lauren checked her e-mails before dinner. She was now amused by her encounter with Josie. For a short while, Lauren had been really worried — until she'd reminded herself that Jennifer was imaginary and only existed because Lauren allowed her to. Lauren had reached the conclusion that Josie had met a pretty girl who fitted Jennifer's description — and simply assumed it was her. The fact that she was also called Jennifer was a coincidence and nothing more.

Lauren's in-box indicated that she had mail, and Lauren clicked it open, wondering if it was Marcus. But the name of the sender suddenly turned her blood to ice.

It was from Jennifer.

With fingers shaking, Lauren opened the message.

Hiya
Spoke to Marcus, he's luvvly. Can't wait 2 meet him. Can u
set something up?
Jxxxxxxxxxxx

Lauren felt sick. What on earth was going on? There was no way Jennifer could have sent Lauren an e-mail. She wasn't even real! Lauren tried to stay calm, but her hands were shaking so much that she couldn't control the mouse. Thought upon thought piled up inside her mind. *If Jennifer didn't send it, then who did? Someone who knows about my double life? Maybe the person hacked into my e-mail account in an attempt to find me out!*

With a hurried click, she deleted the message. If Lauren replied, she was sure that she'd fall into a trap. Who was trying to expose her lie?

"Lauren, dinner!" her mother shouted, and with some relief, Lauren shut off her PC.

"Coming!" she called. As she turned off the light in her room, Lauren thought hard about who could have sent the e-mail from Jennifer. One person was at the top of her list: Chantelle Dawson.

Lauren sat through dinner in silence. Her stomach was churning so hard that she could hardly eat a mouthful. The late nights and talk of Jennifer had left her tired, confused, and edgy. She excused herself from the table and headed for her bed.

But as soon as sleep came, so did a nightmare. This one was even worse than the last. Lauren was at Angie's party, and she was walking through the crowds; now, instead of everyone dancing, they stood staring at her. The music system blared, but they were all silent as the grave. Soon, a sickly sweet fragrance wafted into Lauren's nostrils. She felt like gagging. As she looked for a window to get some fresh air, she saw Jennifer striding up to her. The smell was Jennifer's perfume, and it was overpowering.

"Hi, Lauren — welcome back," she said with an evil sneer ruining her carefully made-up face. And with that, the party exploded into life, but everyone began to dance at a crazy, breakneck pace that made Lauren feel sicker and dizzier.

51

"I have to get out — I'm choking," she said to Jennifer, but her words were drowned out by the heavy, thumping music. Lauren's throat tightened. "I can't breathe! Please help me!" she pleaded, but no one was listening. She saw Marcus nearby, and she ran to him, clutching at his arm. He looked at her without any recognition and shrugged away from her roughly. "Let me out!" she heard herself scream. Jennifer watched from nearby, dancing to the beat, laughing at Lauren.

"You're going to get caught!" she laughed. "Your time is nearly up!"

Lauren desperately struggled to get out. She pushed against the wall of people as hard as she could. She had to get out of this place — away from Jennifer. But everybody refused to budge. Suddenly she felt the pressure of Jennifer's hand around her arm — and the nails sink into her skin. This time it was much more painful.

"Stop it!" she screamed. "Go away! You're not real!"

"I'm part of you now," Jennifer said, gripping her arm even tighter. "I'm *never* going away."

"Jen!" Lauren shouted. "*Jen!*"

She awoke in a cold sweat. Her quilt was on the

floor and her hair was soaked to her forehead. Her mother was standing over her.

"You were screaming in your sleep, honey," her mother said, an anxious look on her face.

"I'm . . . fine, Mom, thanks," Lauren muttered. Her mother gave her a hug, then turned to leave.

"Mom . . . can we talk for a moment?" Lauren asked. But her mother was already gone.

Lauren's door was open a crack, and a sliver of light from the hallway shone in. Her eyes fell upon her arm, and there, unmistakably, was a red hand mark.

Terrified, she got out of bed and hurried to the bathroom. Under the harsh fluorescent glare, she examined her wrist, turning it over underneath the cold water. There were five red marks on her arm — four in a row and one on the underside. Her skin tingled and burned as the water ran over the bruises. *Could I have done this to myself in my sleep?* Lauren thought. As she returned to bed, she couldn't help but feel that things were beginning to slip out of her control.

Lauren decided not to go to Angie's party. It was much easier than having to explain why Jennifer couldn't come. Her dream had really scared her, and Lauren hoped that school might take her mind off everything.

Over the weekend, she thought a lot about the strange e-mail from Jennifer. The more Lauren thought about it, the more she was sure that it must have come from Chantelle. From the very start, it had always been she who'd doubted Lauren's lies.

On Monday morning, Lauren waited for the bus in the cold. There was a large group of her classmates nearby, hopping up and down to keep warm and chatting about their weekend. Lauren wasn't in the mood to get involved, though. As the bus arrived, she stood at the front of the line, desperate to get out of the cold. Chantelle and her friends sat at the back of the bus as usual while Lauren readied herself for a barrage of questions about Jennifer.

"Hey, everybody," she said, nodding at them and trying to look casual.

"Hey," Chantelle and Josie said, nodding back. "Did you hear from Jennifer this weekend?"

Lauren stopped, waiting for the stinging tail at the end of the question. But that's all they said. Lauren chose her words carefully. "Jennifer was busy. So no, I didn't see her," she replied, dumping her schoolbag on the seat next to her.

Josie merely looked disappointed. Chantelle just gave a shrug. There were no comments about e-mails. No sarcastic remarks. Nothing.

Lauren slid quietly into her seat and leaned her head against the window and closed her eyes. Perhaps she had been wrong to suspect Chantelle after all.

Even Marcus sitting down next to her failed to improve her mood. "Hey, Lauren," he said. "I just want to thank you for introducing me to Jennifer. She's such a great girl."

"You've already said," replied Lauren curtly.

"Well, it's true! I can't stop thinking about her — especially after last night."

"Last night?" The comment made Lauren sit up and look at him. "What about last night?"

"We were instant messaging all night. Honestly, Lauren, that girl is so funny and cool. I can't wait to meet her."

"Are you sure?" Lauren asked, staring at him hard. "I mean, are you sure it was last night?"

Marcus frowned. "Of course, I'm sure."

Lauren sat back, feeling numb. *This can't be happening*, she thought. *I didn't go online all weekend.* Lauren began to feel her head spin. As she touched her bruised arm, she felt tears well up in her eyes. *I wish I'd never started any of this.*

As soon as they arrived at school, Lauren grabbed her bag, pushed past Marcus, and ran to the girls' restroom. She was positive that she was going to be sick. She frantically dug around inside her bag. It was time to put an end to the whole nightmare. The Jennifer file would be the first thing to go. She would rip it to shreds and flush it down the toilet. Lauren pulled the folder from her bag and opened it.

It was empty.

She gasped in horror and turned her bag inside out. At the bottom of her bag, a crunched-up piece of paper hit the bathroom floor. She picked it up and opened it.

Hi, Lauren,
Looking for your notes? If you want them back, then you'd better meet me at lunchtime in the art studio.
Chantelle

—

The minutes inched by like hours and finally it was lunchtime. Lauren headed for the art studio. Chantelle was waiting for her when she arrived. To Lauren's absolute dismay, she had brought a crowd with her, including Marcus.

"Well, here she is," Chantelle announced with a smirk. "And I think you're all going to enjoy hearing what Lauren's got to tell us!"

"What are you getting at, Chantelle?" demanded Marcus. "I thought you said we were here about Jennifer."

"Oh, we are," Chantelle said, staring hard at Lauren. "Lauren here is going to tell us all about *Jennifer*, aren't you?"

Lauren was terrified. From the smug look on Chantelle's face, she was sure all her lies about Jennifer were about to be exposed. Lauren would be a complete social outcast. Frantically she tried to think of something plausible to say, but her mind went blank.

"Nothing to say?" said Chantelle, walking toward her. "How about I tell everyone what a liar you are?"

She turned to face everyone. "Lauren's famous friend Jennifer doesn't *exist*."

There was a moment's silence. Then, everyone began to talk among themselves. Lauren's face burned with shame.

"It's not true, right, Lauren?" demanded Marcus. She could see in his eyes that he was hoping desperately Chantelle was wrong.

Lauren's mouth moved silently as she tried and failed to answer.

"Of course, it's true," said Chantelle. "And here's the proof." Out of her bag, Chantelle extracted Lauren's handwritten notes about Jennifer. Lauren could feel the blood draining from her face, and she felt dizzy. This was the worst thing that could have happened: The proof of Lauren's deceit was right there in front of everybody. There was no denying it.

"Excuse me — what's going on?" interrupted a voice in the crowd. It sounded familiar to Lauren, but she couldn't place it. The group opened up to reveal an impossibly beautiful girl with tumbling blonde curls and legs like a racehorse. "Oh, *there* you are, Lauren!" she said. "I've been looking everywhere for you."

The crowd peeled away and let the girl through. She flashed her pretty blue eyes at Marcus.

"You must be Marcus," she said, touching his fingers a tad too long. "You look just like I thought you would."

Marcus stammered incoherently at her.

"Jennifer?" Lauren asked in an incredulous whisper.

The blonde whirled around to face Lauren. "Of course! Who else did you think it was? Now where's my file you were looking after?"

Jennifer took the papers back from Chantelle, whose cheeks were candy-apple red. "Well, I'm so relieved you had my file, Lauren. I've been looking everywhere for it." She nodded at Chantelle and the others. Their faces were a picture of astonishment. "Sorry to dash but nice to meet you all." Jennifer touched Lauren on the arm. It was a warm touch. Then, Lauren smelled something which made her head spin and her throat tighten; it was sickly sweet and flowery. It was the smell of the perfume from Lauren's nightmare.

"I've got to talk to you," Lauren demanded as she went after Jennifer.

Jennifer stopped immediately and beamed. "Of course. What is it you want?"

Lauren looked the girl squarely in the face and hesitated. She knew what she was about to say might sound really, really stupid. "You're not Jennifer," she said. "So who *are* you?"

The girl looked puzzled. "What are you talking about, Lauren? Of course, I'm Jennifer." She motioned to the file. "I was at your house last night, for heaven's sake. You were helping me with my autobiography project for social studies. When I couldn't find it this morning, I figured I must have left it in your bag. So I just dropped by to get it back. I didn't think you'd be upset about it."

Lauren's head was spinning. This couldn't be happening. It was impossible. She tried to protest. "But . . . but you're not even . . . real," she said. "I made you up! You *can't* be here. You can't be Jennifer!" But she knew that what she was saying sounded ridiculous — especially when the proof was standing in front of her.

She swayed dangerously. Jennifer only just managed to stop her from falling to the floor. "Geez, Lauren! Stop acting so weird! We've known each other for years." She helped Lauren steady herself before flashing a concerned smile. "You really ought to go to bed early tonight, you know."

The girl began to head toward the back exit, and Lauren shouted to her. "Where are you going?" she asked.

"Back to school, of course! But I'll see you tonight, Lauren, just like we planned."

And with that, she left the building.

The sensible part of Lauren's brain told her there was no way the girl could have been Jennifer. Surely, it was impossible. . . .

Or was it?

Everything she thought she knew about her world was beginning to blur.

Lauren made her way toward class, wiping tears from her face and trying to pull herself together. *I'll play along with everything for the time being,* she whispered to herself, *but if she turns up again, I'll get right to the bottom of this.*

Lauren didn't have to wait too long. As she turned the corner in the main hallway, she saw a tall, blonde girl waiting outside the principal's office.

"Jennifer?" she gasped.

Jennifer beamed at her.

"I–I thought you'd gone back to your school. . . . " Lauren managed.

Jennifer blushed. "Well, I couldn't tell you the truth, could I? After all, I had to keep things secret until I was a hundred percent sure."

"Sure about what?"

"Well," replied Jennifer with a giggle, "I just saw the principal and had my final interview about switching schools. I start here this afternoon. Now we'll *always* be together, Lauren. Isn't it great?"

Lauren began to back away.

"Where are you going, Lauren?" Jennifer asked, still smiling at her.

"Away from here and away from you!" Lauren screamed, turning to run. But Jennifer was too fast for her.

"Calm down, friend," she said, grabbing Lauren by the arm. Lauren could feel Jennifer's powerful grip and smell the sickening perfume again. Suddenly, she was fighting for breath and she felt weak.

"But . . . you're not real," Lauren said, defeated.

She recognized the look in Jennifer's eyes as she turned to face her. Lauren had seen it before in her nightmare.

"Don't be silly," Jennifer said in a flat, terrifying voice. "I'm more real than you are!"

The rest of the afternoon was a blur. The next thing Lauren knew she was heading home. She was sitting at the front of the bus again, away from the gossip. Her head felt far too fragile to be able to handle it.

It was a massive relief when Lauren finally reached her front door. She looked up and down, and everything seemed normal. For the first time in weeks, Lauren felt like reading some textbooks and doing some homework. She turned the key in the lock.

"Mom! Dad!" she called. *They must be working late*, she thought, as she made her way to the kitchen to make a snack. But as she entered the kitchen, a tall, willowy figure came out of the living room and stood in front of her.

"What are you doing in my house?" Jennifer asked.

Lauren stared at her in horror. "I'm ignoring you," she shouted, throwing her schoolbag on the floor. "I don't know what you're trying to do but this is *my* house and you are *not* real!"

Jennifer didn't move. Instead she folded her arms and smiled in amusement.

It was the smile that Lauren remembered from her nightmare. She felt her throat tighten as she backed away from Jennifer. "You're not real," she said again. "*I'm* the one who thought up *you*! You're just a figment of my imagination."

But Jennifer stepped in front of her, blocking the stairwell. She was still smiling. Lauren closed her eyes. The hot, sweet perfume burned her nostrils.

"I think you'll find it's the other way around, Lauren," Jennifer whispered. "*You're* a figment of *my* imagination."

Lauren's heart thundered so hard against her chest she thought she would faint. She pushed past Jennifer. *I have to get out of here*, Lauren thought frantically. *I have to find my parents and tell them what's going on.* Just then, Lauren heard the key in the front door, and a wave of relief washed over her. Her father was back from work.

"Dad, thank goodness you're home! I've been so —"

Lauren stopped, mid-sentence. Her dad wasn't looking at her.

He seemed to be looking *through* her.

Lauren's father walked over to Jennifer and gave her a big hug. "Jennifer, sweetheart," Lauren heard him say, "were you talking to yourself again? Haven't we discussed this? You're too old to have an imaginary friend."

"You're right, Dad," Jennifer replied. Lauren looked on, mute with terror and confusion. "But don't worry. I'm pretty sure she's gone now . . . forever."

TICKETS, PLEASE

As Brian Magee dribbled the basketball at a lightning-fast pace, he could almost hear the roar of the crowd in his ears. He tossed the ball down the narrow lane bordering the railroad tracks and watched it bounce off the rusty iron fence. His best friend, Craig, caught it before it landed in the tracks.

"Great shot, Magee!" said Craig, dribbling the ball noisily along the tarmac.

Out of nowhere, a thin, wiry girl wearing a sleeveless green-and-yellow basketball shirt darted in front of him and deftly stole the ball with a single, well-timed movement. Brian groaned as he watched her bounce it right down the lane toward the train station, the number seven on her shirt getting smaller and smaller.

"What did you let her do that for?" Brian complained. "We almost won the championships."

"This is *Emily* you're talking about," Craig replied. "If she wasn't a girl, she'd be the best player in the whole school. You try taking the ball from her!"

"I heard that," shouted Emily from the end of the lane. "But it's got nothing to do with me being a girl, Craig. You couldn't take the ball from a kindergartner!"

Brian laughed and tied a green-and-yellow scarf around both wrists. He was well aware of Emily's athletic skills. It was one of the reasons they were such good friends. That and their undying devotion for their city's basketball team. "Yeah, well, *I'm* going to be the best on the team. And if I was playing this afternoon, there would be no stopping me."

Craig nodded enthusiastically. "And we'd be champs!"

"I can't wait to get to the game. Can you?" said Brian. "Seven years since our team last came out on top! They're definitely going to win it today, though. That new guy's been their secret weapon all season long."

"Yeah," agreed Craig. "I just wish they could have played here at home."

Brian shrugged. "Home or away, it makes no difference! History is about to be made."

Emily shouted for them to hurry up. "Come on, you two. If we miss this train, we miss the game. And there's no way we'd be able to walk to the stadium in time!"

Brian broke into a run. "She's right. We'd better get moving. We don't want the train to leave without us."

They roared with excitement and sped down the lane toward the ancient brick building that served as the ticket office.

Today it stood quietly in the summer sunshine, eaves dripping with bright hanging baskets. Emily waited outside, flopped on a wooden bench, her cheeks red with exertion. The ball lay at her feet.

Brian immediately kicked it into the air and began twirling it around.

Emily rummaged in her pockets. "Craig, do you have the cash for the train?"

"I thought you were bringing it!" Craig was looking defensive.

Brian groaned. "I don't believe it! Craig, we *needed*

that money! You said you were going to borrow it from your mom!"

"Sorry, guys," Craig said quietly. "I just totally forgot."

"*Now* what are we going to do?" Emily said, exasperated. "Brian — how much cash do you have?"

Brian considered the change in his pocket. "Umm, along with my ticket for the game, I've got about a buck left over."

"Same here," Craig said glumly.

"Me, too." Emily sighed. "So not one of us has enough for a train ticket. We don't even have time to go all the way back into town to get some cash. What are we going to do? We can't miss the game!"

Brian was serious for a moment. "I've got an idea," he said, suddenly. "Why don't we just forget about the train fare?"

Emily shook her head. "But that's against the law. I mean, what if we get caught?"

"We won't. The game is only a half hour away."

Emily wasn't convinced. "But what do we do when the ticket person asks to see our tickets?"

Brian thought for a moment. "Whenever we've been

to big away games before, we've never been asked to show our tickets. The train's always too crowded."

Craig grinned. "Brian's right. The train is completely chaotic on days like this."

Emily looked doubtful. "And what will we use to bail us out of jail when we're caught?"

"Oh, don't be so melodramatic, Em!" said Craig. "You're always predicting the worst."

"Well, it's a good thing I do. You're such an idiot you never see the downside in any of Brian's plans. That's why both of you are always in detention!"

Brian, sensing a fight, sat down between them on the bench. "Chill out, you two. It's too hot to fight. And besides, it's not as though we'll end up like my great-uncle Ray."

"I didn't know you had a great-uncle Ray," said Emily. "You've never mentioned him."

Brian shook his head. "That's the point. *Nobody* in the family mentions him. It brings back bad memories."

Craig's eyes widened. "Why? What happened?"

"Well," said Brian, "it's a bit of a mystery, really. Great-Uncle Ray was a fan like us and never missed a game. Apparently, the whole thing happened when he was thirteen —"

"That's our age," said Craig.

"Doing better in math, huh, Craig?" Emily said, laughing.

"*Anyway,*" Brian interrupted loudly, "according to my aunt Josie, Great-Uncle Ray took a train from this station and was never seen again!"

"Oh, please," laughed Emily. "How could he just disappear into thin air?"

"It's true," said Brian, his face deadly serious. "When the train arrived at its destination, his big, styrofoam 'Number-One Fan' hand was placed neatly on a seat, but he was nowhere to be found. And no one ever saw him again."

There was silence for a moment before Craig shook his head. "Wow, that's spooky."

"I might have guessed *you'd* believe him, Craig," groaned Emily.

Brian got to his feet. He knew that the trains from this station were always at least ten minutes late but he didn't want to take any chances. They were going to board that train — no matter what.

"Look, I'm going to risk not buying a ticket. Come on — it's only once. . . . Who's with me?"

Craig was immediately at Brian's side, grinning. "I am."

Brian looked pleadingly at Emily. "Oh, come on. It won't be the same without you."

She rolled her eyes and grinned. "OK, I still think you're being an idiot but if you're not paying, then neither am I."

Brian looked at his watch. Their train was due in five minutes, but even though it was such a big day for sports fans, the station was far from packed. In fact, apart from them, it was completely empty.

"It's a little quiet today," whispered Craig.

"Maybe everybody else took an earlier train," suggested Emily. "After all, the game's at two."

But Brian had noticed another person on the platform. The ticket seller was ensconced inside his little wooden booth, reading the newspaper.

"What about him?" he whispered to the others. "We can't risk him seeing us."

Emily drew them into a huddle. "I've thought of that," she said. "We'll creep past him and hide in the waiting room until the train arrives. Then, when the whistle blows, we'll dash out and run on the train as it pulls out."

Brian was impressed. "I thought you weren't a big fan of the idea, Em. Now you're acting like a great train robber!" he joked.

Emily put her hands on her hips. "Are you complaining?"

Brian laughed. "No, no. It's a great idea! Come on, let's go."

They pressed themselves against the station wall and crept, one by one, toward the waiting-room door. As they passed the tiny wooden booth, Brian saw that the ticket seller had his back to them. His feet were up, a newspaper spread out on his lap, and nearby, steam swirled from a coffee mug.

"Nice way to earn a living," whispered Craig. "Drinking coffee and listening to the radio. My dad would love that."

An old-fashioned band tune drifted through the

small round ticket hole in the glass window. Brian stifled a laugh. "Don't think much of his taste in music, though."

"No," agreed Emily. "It's almost as bad as yours!" She stifled a giggle.

Despite their laughter, Brian couldn't help feeling a slight prickle of apprehension. Emily and Craig darted inside the safe walls of the waiting room, but Brian lingered for a moment. Despite the fact the ticket seller still had his back turned, Brian couldn't help feeling the guy was somehow watching him. And there was something about the ticket seller's hair. In the center of the man's bushy black thatch was a bright, almost white streak. It made him look just like a skunk. Brian had never seen anything like it before.

"What are you doing out there?" he heard Emily hiss.

Brian tore himself away and dashed for the door.

The waiting room lay to one side of the platform, a little way up from the ticket seller's small wooden booth and, thankfully, out of his line of sight.

"How much longer is the train going to be?" moaned Craig.

He and Emily settled down to wait on one of the hard wooden benches. Brian passed the time studying the announcements on the waiting-room bulletin board. There was an old yellowing timetable held up by a single rusty nail, a dog-eared advertisement that looked as if it had been there for at least fifty years, and a large notice with a rip down the center. It read:

FAILURE TO TRAVEL WITH A VALID TICKET WILL RESULT IN

The rest of the poster was missing. Brian was just wondering what it might have said, when he heard the unmistakable sound of a train's brakes.

"At last," said Craig, jumping up.

A surge of excitement rushed through Brian's body as he checked the waiting-room window. Another minute or so and they would all be safely on the train.

"It's not a regular train," he reported to the others.

"What do you mean?" asked Craig.

"I mean it's one of those old-fashioned ones with the locking doors. I thought they were taken off the tracks years ago."

Emily pushed her way beside him. "No, they still use them sometimes when the others are being serviced."

A whistle sounded, and it looked as though the train was going to depart. Brian took a deep breath and darted through the waiting-room door. "Come on!" he yelled to Emily and Craig. "Let's go!"

They broke into a run. Brian took the lead and, as they reached the ticket booth, his eyes searched for the ticket seller. Thankfully, he was still inside the booth, hidden behind his newspaper. Brian upped his pace. By the time the old geezer realized what they were up to, it would be miles too late to stop them.

Suddenly, from the corner of his eye, Brian saw the ticket seller rise up in his chair and bang furiously on the glass with his fist.

"Don't you dare get on that train without a ticket!" he roared.

Brian's chest began to pound. The others were right

behind him, but were any of them close enough to make it?

Brian could still hear the ticket seller shouting behind him. "Stop!" he was yelling. "Come back here!"

But it was too late to stop now, and Brian ignored him, bolting at top speed toward the nearest door and grabbing the handle. To his surprise, it refused to budge.

"Hurry up!" yelled Emily, close on his heels.

"Come on, you stupid thing!" Brian shouted at the door. "Open!" He tugged and pulled furiously at the brass handle, but it remained steadfastly shut. "I can't budge it," he said, abandoning his efforts. "I'll try the next one down."

It was a long sprint down the platform, and Brian found himself running alongside a train car packed with passengers. Despite the panic, he couldn't mistake the blur of yellow-and-green basketball shirts pressed against the window. The train began to creak and groan as it moved away from the station.

We're going to win today, Brian thought, *and I'm going to be there to see it!* He reached for the handle on the next car. The ticket seller's shouts were louder now, more urgent.

"You'll be sorry!" he yelled. "Don't say I didn't warn you!"

"Quick — open it," yelled Craig, hot on his heels.

Brian gave the handle a yank, and the door creaked open. The three of them leaped on board and slammed the door firmly behind them, just as the train began to pick up speed.

"How cool was that!" whooped Brian.

"That was so amazing," agreed Emily, trying desperately to catch her breath.

Craig held on to his knees, panting. "It was better than amazing. It was awesome!"

The three of them flopped thankfully down into nearby seats, cheeks red from the chase. Brian took the opportunity to gaze around, noticing how peculiar everything looked. There were open areas, which he was sure were for normal travelers, and old-fashioned compartments with sliding doors.

"I've just had a terrible thought," Emily said. "We *are* on the right train, aren't we?"

The grin left Brian's face. In all the excitement he

hadn't thought to check. "This has to be the right train. I noticed a section full of fans."

"Did you hear that ticket seller shouting at us?" giggled Emily. "I thought he was going to blow a gasket he was so angry."

"I know," agreed Brian. "It was a close one."

"The door handle was a bit of a challenge, though," said Emily, feeling the mock leather seats with her hand. "These old trains are really strange, aren't they? Even the seats are weird." She shifted about uncomfortably. "I'm glad we're only going a few stops."

Brian explored the small compartment they were in. "It reminds me of an old black-and-white film I saw once. Everyone was sitting in a cubicle just like this when the train went through a tunnel. Anyway, when they came out of the other side, one of the passengers was missing. All that was left was an empty seat. It creeped me out. They spent the rest of the film looking for the body."

Craig stood on his seat and reached inside the large shelf above their heads. "Did they find it up here?" he asked.

Brian got up beside him. "No, that's for luggage."

Craig grinned. "I *know*. My grandpa used to work every day on a train like this. He talks about it all the time, now that he's retired. He says these old models were much more reliable than the newer ones."

"You don't get these compartments on modern trains, either," said Emily, rolling their basketball beneath a seat for safekeeping. "I think it's nicer. Kinda like traveling in your own little room."

They slid open a glass door and peered out. A central corridor ran the full length of the car ahead. Craig got up and went off to investigate.

"Should he be doing that?" Emily asked. "I mean, haven't we taken enough risks already? We don't want to get caught now."

"Relax, Em," Brian said, trying his best to reassure her. "I'm sure it'll be fine."

Craig called out excitedly from the other end of the car. "Hey, guys, feast your eyes on this! It's a first-class compartment. Feel like traveling in style today?"

"Yeah!" cried Brian, heading eagerly along the corridor. He'd hardly made it through the door before Emily caught him by the arm.

"Look," she said seriously. "There could be a guard on board."

They heard Craig's voice boom impatiently from the end of the corridor. "Did you see how empty the station was?" He rolled his eyes in exasperation. "If there are no passengers, then *of course* there won't be any guards. Why don't you both just relax!"

To Brian's relief, Emily managed a smile. "You're probably right," she said. "Our team probably travels first-class all of the time, so why shouldn't their fans?"

"Now you're talking!" said Brian, giving her a gentle shove down the aisle.

"You two need to chill," advised Craig, waiting for them at the door. "I mean, can you see any guards on this train?"

Brian and Emily shook their heads.

"Exactly. There aren't even any other passengers in this entire car. So we can sit where we want. Nobody's going to catch us, OK!" He slid back the first-class door with a flourish. "Now, after you!"

Brian was first to step inside. "Wow," he breathed, as he gazed around the old compartment.

The seats in the car were deep and squishy and upholstered in velvety red fabric. The walls were paneled with rich walnut, and even the luggage rack was inlaid with polished wood.

"*This* is the life," said Brian, sinking into his seat with his hands behind his head.

There was a *clonk*, as Craig fiddled with a catch beneath the window and released a small folding table. He pulled at a wooden toggle. The blind snapped back into its housing with a crack.

"Amazing!" Emily said.

"Told you it was a good idea," Brian said.

She smiled and leaned her head against the velvet headrest. "OK, I admit it. You were right. It was an excellent idea."

Excellent. Brian smiled. That was just how he felt at this moment. He was riding first-class on a train beside his two best friends, and soon he would be sitting in the stadium watching his favorite team.

Suddenly, Brian sat bolt upright in his seat. He motioned to the others to be quiet. "Did either of you hear that?"

"Hear what?" asked Craig.

"Music or something," said Brian. "I swear I heard something."

Brian, Craig, and Emily stopped talking for a moment and listened intently. There it was. A creepy, high-pitched tune.

"You mean that kind of whistling?" said Craig, chewing his lip uncertainly.

Brian nodded. By now, the unmistakable sound of whistling was drifting up the corridor toward them.

"Who do you think it is?" Craig said. "Do you think it's an inspector?"

"I think I'm going to be sick," said Emily, closing her eyes.

Brian tried to find some words of reassurance but failed. The thin, reedy notes echoing through the corridor reminded him of nasty, old-fashioned, wind-up jack-in-the-box tunes. He gave an involuntary shudder as he thought back to the brightly painted jack-in-the-box he'd been given for his fourth birthday. It had made him hate clowns for ever afterward. Other kids were afraid of the dark, but Brian hated that clown — the way it would jump out, its face leering. Not to mention that slow and awful tune. He glanced around. Even Craig looked fearful. Brian didn't know why, but that whistling was creeping him out.

The whistling sounded like it was just outside in the corridor.

He glanced through the window, and his blood froze. There, reflected in the long car window, was the ticket inspector. From the angle where Brian was sitting, he could see that the old man was still a little way down the main car, but he would be coming closer very soon.

Craig and Emily seemed to see him at the same moment.

"He's almost here!" hissed Craig. "What should we do?"

"Quick," Brian whispered, looking desperately in every direction. "Hide!"

"But there's nowhere to hide. . . . We're trapped!" Emily said. "There's only one way out and that's into the corridor."

"We're done for," hissed Craig, panicking.

They all heard the slow, heavy footsteps making their way up the corridor toward their compartment, accompanying the eerie whistling.

Brian's eyes desperately scanned the small compartment in vain, trying to find a safe place to hide. The sound of the inspector's shoes on the hard corridor floor grew louder.

In desperation, Brian dived for the floor. "Quick," he urged. "Get as low as you can and press yourselves up against the door. Hopefully he'll look in but not down."

"I told you this was a terrible idea," whispered Emily angrily. "We should have bought a ticket. Now he'll toss us off the train."

Craig groaned. "It's miles. It'll take us *ages* to walk."

Brian was silent. Skipping the fare had seemed harmless enough when he'd come up with the idea earlier. He hadn't considered that they might get caught.

The footsteps were so close now that Brian could feel their vibration through the train floor. The whistling was getting louder and louder. He tried not to think about how there was only a thin sliding door between them and the ticket inspector.

Just then, the footsteps and the whistling stopped.

Brian held his breath as he realized the ticket inspector was right outside the door.

Beside him, Emily and Craig stiffened, and his own

mind raced as he tried not to imagine the inspector's face peering in through the compartment window. The silence seemed to stretch on forever.

Why didn't the man leave? Brian's heart was pounding now. What was taking him so long? It could only mean one thing: He was on to them. Any second now, they would feel the compartment door slide back and trouble would start.

But suddenly, to Brian's relief, the footsteps started up again. This time, they were heading away from the door toward the front of the car. The ticket inspector was leaving. Brian was so grateful he could hardly speak. He looked at his friends in triumph. They had gotten away with it!

W ell, we can't stay in this compartment," said Emily, straightening her basketball shirt. "There's nowhere to hide, and we are bound to get caught. We should go to where the other fans are, or somewhere where it's less exposed."

"Emily's right," Brian said, standing up. "We can't stay here and get caught. We'll have to split up. That way it'll be easier to hide. Then, just before the train pulls into our station, we'll meet up in the front car. You know, the one just behind the conductor."

Emily nodded in agreement. "I'll head for the guard's car, where they store the luggage and bicycles and stuff. There's bound to be a place to hide in there."

"Good idea," said Brian. "You go the same way as Em, Craig. I'll stand in the corridor and keep an eye out while you make your move."

He slid the compartment door back and slipped into the passageway. To his relief it was totally empty. "Coast's clear," he whispered. "But I think you'd better head that way. The guard's area is always at the back of the train."

Emily and Craig disappeared along the corridor while Brian's eyes darted nervously from one end of the car to the other, checking for danger signs. They'd almost reached the adjoining car's door when Emily shot him a final glance over her shoulder.

"Go on," he hissed. "Just go!"

Without the others, the car seemed deathly silent to Brian. His stomach was making knots, and he felt completely exposed. He couldn't understand why, but the sound of the whistling and the footsteps had completely unnerved him. It all just felt . . . *wrong*.

Brian gripped the side of the compartment door and took a deep breath. He was just wondering where he could hide when he felt a burst of pain in his fingertip. He snatched his hand away from the paneled door. A splinter of wood poked out from underneath his nail and a small drop of blood oozed in a crimson blob. Brian examined the compartment door carefully. He noticed a set of initials carved into the wood: R.M. Brian sucked his finger angrily. It looked as if the letters had been hacked into the frame, probably with a penknife. It had been left rough around the edges, that was why he'd caught his finger on it. As he rummaged in his pocket for a tissue, the sound of whistling filled the air once more.

The ticket taker couldn't be back again already? Brian fixed his eyes on the door. *Wait a minute*, Brian thought. *Wasn't that the same direction the guy came from last time? How can that be?* Brian was sure he'd heard him exit the corridor the other way. It didn't make sense.

The whistling was louder now, and Brian felt his

mind go into overdrive. Perhaps the inspector had doubled back past their car without them noticing. He shook his head. *No, it was impossible.* Craig and Emily had made their escape immediately after the inspector had disappeared from sight.

Whatever the explanation, this wasn't the time to make sense of it. He had to find a place to hide — and fast. As quick as a flash, he darted down the corridor and dived into the compartment, pulling the door tightly shut behind him. Once inside, he jumped up onto the seat and scrambled into the only available hiding place: the overhead luggage rack. It was a tight squeeze, and Brian had to force his way onto the ledge and lie with his nose pressed up against the ceiling. He wondered if he'd ever manage to struggle out again.

The sound of footsteps, slow and heavy, made their way along the corridor toward his compartment, and Brian wished that Emily and Craig were still with him. The footsteps stopped. Once again, the ticket inspector lingered outside the compartment door. Surely nobody could spot him up here? Brian felt his forehead turn sweaty. And in that instant, an overwhelming urge gripped him. He wanted to peek — to stare over the edge and get a good look at the man who whistled annoying tunes. The feeling took such a sharp hold of him that before he had time to think about the risk, Brian had slid to the edge of the luggage shelf and craned his neck over the edge.

The ticket inspector was walking away, and Brian only managed to catch sight of the back of his head. It was more than enough. Brian threw himself back, tight to the wall, his heart racing. There was only one other person he'd ever seen in his life with that hair — jet-black with a pure white streak down the middle. Just like a skunk, he'd thought at the time. But it *couldn't* be the ticket seller. It was impossible. He hadn't even left his booth.

As the footsteps drifted away, Brian wondered what to do. Should he go and find Craig and Emily and tell them? They might think that he was crazy. Surely it'd be worth riding out the weirdness. After all, they were only going a couple of stops. But doubts still ate away at him. Something about this train wasn't right. Not right at all.

Brian realized he'd become unbearably hot. He wriggled uncomfortably on the hard wood. It had seemed a good idea at the time, the three of them splitting up, but now he wasn't so sure. The isolation had started to make him anxious, and he was beginning to get angry at being so scared of some old ticket inspector. He had had enough. He decided to go and find Craig and Emily, or at least to find the compartment full of fans that he had seen from the station earlier.

He struggled down from the luggage shelf and crept into the corridor. Thankfully it was clear. There wasn't another soul in sight — and no noise, either. Brian felt a sense of unease. During the whole time on the train, they had all been so preoccupied with getting caught, it had never occurred to Brian that he hadn't seen a single other passenger.

Not one.

Curious, he made his way along the length of the corridor, peering into every compartment along the way.

They were all empty.

Weird, he said to himself. *Still, it should be different in the next car.* It had to be. He reached for the handle of the adjoining door, certain that it would be full of stadium

91

chants and noisy chatter. He'd see Craig and Emily singing along with everyone else.

He stepped inside and looked around. It, too, was empty.

There was no noise, no litter, and no people. Brian was utterly alone. And then he heard something that made him freeze.

The sound of whistling and footsteps.

A lump like a stone rose up in Brian's throat. He willed himself to run, but his whole body was bound by terror. As the low, unearthly sound filled the corridor, he somehow felt the cheerful little tune was mocking him. For what seemed like eternity, Brian stood helplessly in the corridor trying to decide which direction the inspector would appear from next. Where could he hide when he didn't even know which way to run?

Brian spotted a door beside him. It was different from the rest — solid from top to bottom with no glass window. He pushed it open and darted inside. He'd managed to find the restroom — and restrooms *always* had locks.

Immediately, he shot the bolt and, stepping backward, nearly fell over the toilet bowl. Recovering a little, he glanced around. The room was tiny, the toilet and washbasin swallowing all the available space. He was sure that he could feel the temperature rise and he was sweating even more, but this time the sweat was cold and clinging.

The ticket inspector was inside the car now, Brian was sure of that. He could hear the long, slow footsteps striding along the corridor toward him. They were at odds with Brian's heart, which pumped so fast inside his chest, he worried the inspector might hear.

The footsteps halted on the other side of the door. The whistling stopped abruptly. *He'll leave in a minute*, Brian chanted inside his head. *He'll leave in a minute. Please make him leave in a minute.*

Brian watched in horror as the handle began to move. His chest suddenly tightened, and he pulled uncomfortably at the neck of his basketball shirt.

The handle rattled again. Brian wedged a foot beneath the door and grasped the lock hard with both hands. It shook violently, but he closed his eyes and held on tight.

And then the pressure on the handle stopped. The

whistling and the footsteps receded once more. Brian looked down at his hands: They were red and sore. He slumped onto the toilet seat, wiping his sweaty forehead with the bottom of his shirt.

After a moment, Brian rose shakily to his feet and gathered himself in the mirror. He smoothed down his hair and splashed cold water on his face.

Come on, Magee, he told himself as he stared in the mirror. *What are you so afraid of? The worst he can do is to throw you off the train!*

He took a deep breath and reached for the lock, but then he pulled his hand away as though the handle were red-hot. The initials R.M. were carved into the door frame. Brian touched the jagged carving with his fingers. They were rough around the edges, like the ones he'd snagged his finger on in the first-class compartment. But when he looked a little closer, he could see that the wood had begun to discolor, which might have meant that the scratches had been made a long time ago.

He wondered briefly who R.M. was. The carvings reminded Brian of one of those nature trails where the route was carved into stumps along the way. It was almost as if he was following in this R.M.'s footsteps along the train. The thought suddenly made him shiver, and he tried to shake it off. Brian reached for the door handle, his mind made up. Being alone on this train was way too creepy. He had to go find Craig and Emily.

The moment Brian left the tiny room, he formed a plan. As soon as he found Craig and Emily, they'd stick together and get off the train — even if they were nowhere near the station they wanted.

But they must have had the same idea as Brian because as he shut the toilet door he heard them behind him.

"Craig, Emily!" Brian yelled. "Over here!" It was obvious from their pale faces and pinched expressions that something was very wrong.

"I cut my arm," Emily said.

"How did you do that?" Brian asked.

"It was just now, when me and Craig were making our way toward the front to find you."

"Yeah," nodded Craig, his cheeks still pale and shocked. "We were in the luggage car down there, when the ticket inspector came. I had to duck behind some suitcases. I thought he'd seen me, but he just walked past. It was a close call."

"And I managed to squeeze between a couple of weird-looking antique bikes," explained Emily. "He didn't spot me, either, but there was a sharp edge on one of the mudguards. It scratched my arm."

Brian nodded. "I saw him make his way down there just now. I wondered if you'd manage to get out of the way in time."

"What about you?" asked Craig. "Where did you hide?"

"It's a long story, but let's just say I'm feeling pretty weirded out. The guy just seemed to keep coming and coming. Even though I tried to figure out where I'd last seen him, he always seemed to turn up in the opposite direction."

Emily nodded in agreement. "And his hair, too! Did you see it?"

"With a white stripe down the back," said Craig. "Just like a —"

"— skunk," Brian finished. "It was exactly the same as the ticket seller's hair back at the station. I remember seeing it."

Emily stared hard at Brian. "Well, there couldn't be two people with such weird hair, right?"

Craig rubbed his head in agitation. "We need to get off, that's all I know. I won't be happy until I've left this train!"

"But that's the whole point," Emily said anxiously. "How can we leave, when that man's everywhere?"

"We'll have to take a chance, that's all," Brian told the others. "If we stay where we are, it won't be long before he's back."

"Where are we going?" asked Craig, as he followed Brian's lead.

"To the first passenger car up front," Brian said determinedly. "If we're up there, at least we know where he'll be coming from. We could always block the door or something."

Brian led his friends forward. Despite his brave words, his heart was thumping out of his chest. "Coast's clear," he whispered, trying to hide his relief each time he opened a door.

Eventually, they made it to the front car. Like all the others, it was old-fashioned and seemed to be empty. They'd barely had time to close the door behind them when Craig gave a shout. "We're slowing down!" he cried, rushing toward a sliding window.

Brian felt himself grinning. "Look," he said, pointing at a long steel shed beside them. "That's the engine shed. We must be coming into the station."

Sure enough, the tarmac of the platform suddenly ran along beside them and Craig whooped with joy. "Yes!" he shouted. "We're going to make it. We're actually going to make it. We are going to get off this train at last! I take back everything I said about you earlier, Magee. You're a genius!"

Emily managed a smile. "More like lucky," she said, shaking her head.

"Hang on . . . wait a minute! Listen . . ." said Brian.

Emily looked desperately at him. "No way! Not now!"

The sound of whistling grew suddenly louder, and now they could hear the ticket inspector's footsteps, too. The floor felt as though it was rattling with the inspector's footfalls.

"He's just behind the door!" yelled Craig, terrified.

Emily threw her body against the adjoining door

and grabbed the handle hard. "Craig," she shouted. "Come help me hold the door. We'll keep him out until we reach the station. Get ready to run!"

The handle began to rattle on the other side as Emily and Craig hung on for dear life.

"We're pulling in!" Brian shouted. "Hold on!" He tugged at the brass handle on the exit door.

It refused to budge.

I don't believe this, Brian said to himself, and he tried the handle once again.

"Hurry up!" shrieked Emily from the end of the car. "We can't hold him much longer."

The whistling seemed relentless now. It filled the entire car, the shrill melody assaulting Brian's ears, making it hard for him to think. He could see groups of passengers crowding along the platform. Brian began to bang on the glass with both fists. "Please help us! I can't open the door! We have to get off!"

"What's going on?" yelled Craig, angrily. "Get that door open!"

"I'm trying!" Brian replied, still banging and shouting. "But it's completely stuck, so I'm trying to get help."

Nobody on the platform seemed to even glance toward the train. In fact, nobody took any notice. It was as if they couldn't see him.

Or the train.

"Please," Emily begged. "You *have* to get it open, Brian. We can't last much longer!"

Suddenly, Brian noticed a small, angular figure seated in the corner. It was an elderly passenger. Had he been there all along? Perhaps he could help them.

"Excuse me, but we're —"

Brian stopped speaking as he saw for the first time what the man was doing. Brian's body trembled as his eyes moved to the old man's hands. Thin, knotted fingers wielded a penknife. Through the whistling, Brian seemed to be able to hear the scrape of metal on wood as the blade etched a scar into the paneling near the man's seat. Brian saw the deep curves of the letter R already finished. Now the old man was working carefully on the M.

Brian's eyes were locked on that letter. "M," he read.

M for Magee.

Terror flooded Brian's vision. As he looked around,

he saw for the first time that this car was different from the others. The wooden floor, the paneled walls, and even the ceiling were covered in carved letters.

Thousands of carved letters.

All of them read R.M.

"U-Uncle Ray?" Brian stammered, as Emily and Craig stared in disbelief. "Is that you?"

Slowly, the man's wizened cheeks turned to face him. His mouth twisted into a thin smile. "You should have bought a ticket, son," he said in a hollow, cracked voice.

Brian's arms fell helplessly to his sides. The whole car fell eerily silent as the train picked up speed along the track.

Silent except for a soft, low whistling right behind him . . .

KILLING TIME

Alexis Leigh flopped down on her bed and idly thumbed the pages of a magazine.

It was Saturday morning, and Alexis's best friends, Amber and Tori, had dropped by for their usual make-over session. Every week, they would attempt to transform one of themselves into a celebrity from the pages of their favorite magazine.

Amber had received some crimping irons for her birthday and couldn't wait to try them out. So when Tori volunteered to be her model, Amber was delighted. While the two girls grappled inexpertly with the steaming plates, Alexis was content with playing the role of stylist. She lay on her tummy, chin in hands, advising Amber and Tori from the comfort of her bed.

"Don't brush it, that's all I'm saying," Alexis said.

"Why not?" Tori asked, wincing slightly as Amber just missed her earlobe with the hot curling irons. "Why shouldn't I brush it?"

"Will you just please sit still?" Amber said in frustration. "I've nearly finished. I'm on the bangs."

"Leave the bangs, Amber," Alexis advised in an earnest voice. "You don't want to overdo it."

Amber leaned over the top of Tori's head and stared at her. "Are you sure?"

"I'm sure," Alexis said. She reached over and loaded a CD into her stereo, grabbing a tube of potato chips from the dresser. "Plus it's snack time. Care for a cheese-and-chive Pringle?"

As the CD began to play, Amber unplugged the curling irons and joined Alexis on the bed. She helped herself to a chip. "Hey — I love this song! I didn't know you had it."

Alexis grinned. "You can borrow it if you like."

They sang along while Tori admired her new look

in the mirror. "It's great, but why did you tell me not to brush it?"

Alexis noticed Tori and Amber looking at her and seized her chance. She pushed three chips in her mouth sideways. "Because . . ." She stopped as her eyes began to water. "Because . . ."

"Alexis?" said Tori, looking up from the dresser. "Are you all right?"

But Alexis didn't answer. Instead, her eyes widened, and her throat began to tighten. She clutched at her chest and began to heave.

"She's choking!" shrieked Amber. "What do we do?"

The heaving turned to gasping, and Alexis began to grab at the bedspread, writhing and jerking. She shot them a desperate look before sliding heavily to the floor.

"Look, look. Her face is turning purple!" Amber shrieked.

Immediately, Tori dropped to her knees and began slapping Alexis's shoulder blades hard. "Quick, Amber, bang her on the back!"

The girls watched in horror as Alexis slumped downward and lay motionless on the carpet. There was a moment's shocked silence, then they heard footsteps on the stairs outside the door.

The bedroom door rattled and a head appeared.

"Only me, girls. Just to tell you —" Alexis's mom stopped mid-sentence. "Is something wrong?"

Wordlessly, Tori and Amber stood back to reveal Alexis's body slumped on the carpet.

"We don't know how it happened, Mrs. Leigh," Amber began. "We were just . . . doing our hair, you know . . . and then Alexis . . . snacks . . ." Her sentence descended into nothing.

There was an awkward silence, and then someone giggled.

"Gotcha!" Alexis said, snapping her eyes open. She clambered to her feet and took a bow.

"Alexis!" gasped Tori and Amber at the same time.

"You didn't believe I was really dead, did you?" Alexis laughed. "I was only acting."

Tori shoved Alexis in the arm. "You scared me, you idiot!"

"Sorry, T," Alexis said sheepishly. "So . . . I guess I got it right, no?"

"That was *awesome*, Al!" Amber said. "Tori and me . . . well, we thought you were in serious trouble."

"Honestly?" Alexis said, glowing with pride. "Was I really that good?"

"Absolutely," nodded Tori. "You had us fooled. My heart's still thumping like crazy!"

"Well, I don't think that was funny at all," said Mrs. Leigh.

Still, it was exactly the response Alexis had been hoping for, because tomorrow the three girls had drama class and their teacher, Miss LaSalle, had promised the class a game called Wink Murder. Right away, Alexis had realized this was the perfect opportunity to impress her. Alexis's lifelong dream was to become a famous actress, and Miss LaSalle had important connections in the showbiz world. She had been an actress herself and even starred in a movie — although it hadn't done very well in theaters. Every summer, Miss LaSalle took two of her most promising pupils to a theater workshop, where famous actors would occasionally lead training sessions. This year, Alexis was determined to be one of those chosen.

Alexis smiled and reached for the empty Pringles

tube lying on the carpet. "What can I say?" she began in an elegant accent, holding the tube to her cheek like an Oscar statuette. "If it wasn't for the support of my friends, and of course my mother's healthy cooking, I wouldn't be accepting this award today. . . ."

Mrs. Leigh smiled. "Time to come back to the real world now, Alexis. Tori's mom is waiting outside in her car."

Alexis shrugged at Amber and Tori. "Everyone's a critic."

After waving good-bye to Tori and Amber, Alexis followed her mother into the kitchen. "*Because* you're the best mom ever," she began, "do you think you might do me a small favor?"

Mrs. Leigh looked up from loading the washing machine. "Look, Alexis, if you want me to wash your jeans, then you'd better hurry up and bring them down to me. This is the only dark load I'm doing tonight."

Alexis shook her head. "No, Mom, it's nothing like that. I just want you to wink at me from time to time."

Mrs. Leigh smoothed a curl from her forehead and frowned. "You've lost me."

"Wink. You know." She attempted a wink with her left eye, but didn't quite succeed.

"Sometimes I wonder about you, Alexis," Mrs. Leigh said, reaching for the laundry detergent.

"But this is homework, Mom — honestly. It's for drama class. We're playing a game of Wink Murder tomorrow, and I want to make sure I'm totally prepared," Alexis explained.

"Wink Murder?" Her mom tilted her head to one side and stared at Alexis, as if to say, "What are you talking about?"

Alexis knew that she'd have to start at the beginning. "Listen — Wink Murder's a game we play in drama class. Everybody sits in a circle and closes their eyes. Then Miss LaSalle picks someone out and taps them on the back."

"Miss LaSalle?"

"*Yes*, she's our drama teacher," Alexis replied impatiently. "Anyway, the person she chooses gets to be the murderer, understand? And because everyone has their eyes closed, they don't know who that person is. They just have to wait to be killed."

Alexis's mom shook her head. "So how does the murderer kill everybody, then?"

"By winking at them, of course," Alexis replied.

"But you've all got your eyes closed. How would you see?"

"We've *opened* them again by now. Try to keep up, Mom. Anyway, if you get winked at — and this is the best part — you have to die in the most dramatic way possible."

"And what happens when everyone's dead? It all sounds a little pointless to me," her mom said, turning back to the washing machine.

"No, you don't understand. It's the detective's job to stand in the middle of the circle and identify the murderer before everyone in the class gets killed."

"But you didn't say there was a detective."

Alexis was exasperated now. "*OK*, so I left that part out. Miss LaSalle chooses somebody to be a detective at the start of the game." Alexis stopped to take a deep breath. "But the point is this: We've got class tomorrow, and I want my death to be the best out of everybody's."

"Well — if it'll help, then I suppose I can wink

at you once in a while." Her mom gave Alexis a big wink.

"Arrgh," Alexis groaned, and collapsed to the floor.

Despite the fact it was an overcast Monday morning, Alexis felt really cheerful. "I can't wait for drama," she said to Amber as they made their way toward school.

"I can't wait to see you try out that dying routine on the others — it really shook me up!" Amber replied.

Up ahead, Alexis could see Tori waiting for them. She was wearing a big hat.

Alexis sighed as she approached Tori. "You brushed it, didn't you?"

Tori gave her a sheepish look. "Well, I didn't think it would be that big a deal . . . but look at what's happened." She removed her hat to reveal a huge mess of frizzy hair.

"I told you not to! You're just supposed to comb it through with your fingers or it goes —"

"— crazy," finished Tori.

Amber tilted her head. "Actually, it's not that bad," she said loyally. "I mean big hair is really in at the moment, right, Alexis?"

Alexis nodded, trying hard not to laugh.

Tori managed a small smile. "Really?"

"Absolutely." Alexis avoided her gaze, afraid she might burst out laughing and hurt Tori's feelings. "Anyway, look on the bright side: It will eventually go back to normal and it doesn't look nearly as bad as when Amber dyed her hair last year."

"Hey! I thought that looked pretty cool!" Amber said indignantly. Alexis and Tori began to hoot with laughter.

Suddenly, there were footsteps behind them. Alexis turned, and she immediately felt her smile fade. It was Jordan Franklin, a boy with all the charm of a spitting cobra. Alexis remembered the time two years ago when she'd tried to be friends with him. Even now the whole thing still made her shudder. He had been nice to her for a while, and Alexis had even started to like him. But in a single moment everything had changed.

It was a math test that did it. Jordan hadn't studied and insisted on sitting next to Alexis so he could copy her work. She'd refused, and that was when she saw the other side of Jordan Franklin.

First, he stopped talking to her. However, that wasn't

a problem, Alexis could handle that. Then other things started happening. Cruel things.

Her locker was broken into and her math notebook soaked with water. Then the straps on her schoolbag were cut and slashed with scissors. She had told the math teacher what had happened — only to find that she didn't believe Alexis's story. Soon after, Alexis discovered her cell phone on the floor. It had "dropped" out of her backpack, and the screen was broken. But she could never prove that Jordan was to blame for any of it.

But it had been the mouse that disturbed her the most. Somebody had placed it inside the hood of her jacket, its tiny body crawling down Alexis's arm before it escaped through the sleeve.

Even the teacher shrieked several times before chasing it away. "Who did it?" she had demanded. "Which individual in this class is sick enough to do such a thing?"

Nobody had answered, but Jordan gave Alexis the tiniest of smiles. It was so small that only she noticed.

But it had been enough.

Since then, she had avoided Jordan whenever

possible. Other kids in her class had experienced similar things when they had problems with him, though nothing as severe. Mostly, they'd come back to their lockers to see that the metal doors had been kicked in or written on in thick permanent marker. Or sometimes their textbooks were torn to pieces and strewn down the hallway. But Jordan was always too clever to get caught. He had one friend — a boy named Adam Moran — who had all the intelligence of a caveman. For some reason that Alexis could never quite fathom, he worshipped the ground Jordan Franklin walked on. Wherever he went, Adam followed with the same stupid grin plastered across his clueless-looking face.

More recently, Jordan had invited Tori to the Winter Dance, but she had said no. Alexis had stiffened when Tori had told her. If a trivial thing like a math test could lead to all kinds of trouble, Alexis wondered what a personal rejection might do.

She watched wordlessly as Jordan approached, an uncomfortable feeling rising in the pit of her stomach. Not for the first time, he reminded Alexis of a rottweiler: cruel and tenacious. He licked his thin lips as he headed toward Tori. In that instant, Alexis knew there was going to be trouble.

"*Someone's* having a bad hair day!" he began with a sneer. "What happened, Tori? Did you get plugged into an electrical outlet?"

"Go away, lizard boy," snapped Amber.

Jordan made a sullen face and sobbed sarcastically. "How could you be so mean to me?"

"Oh — pretty easily," Amber replied coolly.

Alexis shot a look at Tori, who was already visibly upset by Jordan's antics.

He turned his attention back to Tori. "So . . . is this a new thing? The Viking look? Will you also grow a beard and invade small villages? Oops, sorry, I can see you've begun the beard thing already." He and Adam laughed loudly.

Tori's face crumpled. Jordan really seemed to be enjoying himself. Alexis was furious. *How can he be so mean?* Anger began to rise up inside her. Tori was the nicest person she knew. Jordan had no right to give her such a hard time just because she wouldn't go to a stupid dance with him. Alexis decided to take action. "OK, that's it, I've had enough —"

"Please don't, Alexis," Tori said, grabbing her arm. "I'd rather forget about it."

"Yeah, everyone already knows that Adam and Jordan are losers," agreed Amber, her cheeks flushed with anger.

The girls linked arms and headed into school.

"I wouldn't take the main entrance, Tori," shouted Jordan after them. "You might frighten some of the younger kids!"

Alexis watched Tori turn around. *Oh, no*, she thought.

"I know *exactly* why you're doing all this," Tori said evenly. She looked Jordan in the face. "It's because I wouldn't go to the Winter Dance with you, right?"

Jordan shrugged. "I don't know what you're talking about. I was just being honest about your hair and stuff. No need to get upset."

But Alexis could see Tori was past being upset. She was so angry, she was actually shaking.

"Well, now *I'm* being honest," Tori went on. "If you think I'd ever go *anywhere* with a creep like you, then you're sorely mistaken."

Jordan staggered back in mock horror. "Ooh," he said, gripping his chest. "I'm wounded. You're killing me!"

Adam guffawed loudly, enjoying the joke. *Death would be too kind*, thought Alexis.

But Tori wasn't finished yet. When she spoke again, her voice was like steel. She walked over to Jordan and smiled. "Do you know something?" she said as cool as a cucumber. "I nearly said yes when you asked, but I realized I didn't know you well enough. In fact, I was going to give it a week and invite *you* to a movie instead."

For the first time ever, Alexis saw Jordan look uncertain. His whole demeanor suddenly changed. If she wasn't mistaken, he looked flattered.

"Really?" he said, his cheeks flushing with pleasure. "You were going to ask me out?"

Tori put her face close to his, and Alexis thought for one insane moment that she was actually serious — until Tori burst out laughing.

"As if!" Tori said with a wicked laugh. "As if I'd ever hang out with a dweeb like you!" Tori turned away. "And by the way," she said as a parting shot, "with breath like yours, a mint wouldn't hurt!"

There was a moment's absolute silence. Some older

girls had been passing by, and Alexis watched with satisfaction as they pointed and laughed at Jordan. His cheeks glowed scarlet with humiliation.

"Tori, that . . . was . . . AMAZING," said Alexis, bursting into laughter.

"Genius, sheer genius!" agreed Amber, grinning widely.

They walked off arm in arm, still laughing. Behind them, Jordan thumped Adam in the arm and shouted something at them, but it was lost in the chatter of the playground.

Alexis couldn't help shuffling impatiently as Miss LaSalle addressed the class.

"Now — as I've told you all before," she said, "a good actor never acts. He, or she, merely *reacts*." Miss LaSalle paused, and made sure that everyone was paying attention. "Wink Murder may be only a game, but it's also a very valuable exercise in some of the more basic acting skills. . . ."

Alexis was only half listening. "I hope I'm not the murderer," she whispered excitedly.

Amber looked at her. "Why's that?"

"Can't wink," replied Alexis seriously. She gave Amber and Tori a quick demonstration.

"Pathetic," giggled Amber. "That was more like a blink!"

Alexis shrugged. "Happens every time," she said. "I've tried practicing but I still can't do it. It's like one of my eyelids won't work without the other one."

Amber grasped her by the shoulders and looked her squarely in the face. "It's easy," she said. "Copy me."

Tori gave a giggle. "If you two could see yourselves!"

"Shh," said Amber. "This is serious. OK, Alexis, look me in the eye. Now relax and clear your mind. Try to think about something other than winking."

"Like what?" asked Alexis, who couldn't think about anything *except* winking now.

"I don't know," said Amber. "Use your imagination. Now, when I give the signal, just relax and let your eyelid go. Don't give it too much thought, just copy me, OK?"

Alexis nodded.

"Great," said Amber. "Now on the count of three. One . . . two . . . three . . . wink!"

"How did I do?" asked Alexis.

Tori and Amber looked at each other.

"Still a blink, I'm afraid," Amber said.

"I'd stick to dying if I were you," said Tori diplomatically.

"Just keep practicing," Amber added. "If you remember what I've told you, you'll soon be able to give the perfect killer wink!"

"I prefer the dying part anyway," shrugged Alexis, her mind turning back to the theater workshop.

Miss LaSalle clapped her hands together for silence. "It is time," she announced, "for a murderer to be found. Let's move our chairs into a circle."

Amid the din of scraping chairs, Jordan and Adam approached Alexis, Amber, and Tori. Alexis braced herself for the backlash from Tori's earlier outburst. But considering his earlier humiliation, Jordan looked surprisingly calm.

"What do *you* want?" demanded Amber, scowling.

"Girls," Jordan said, holding up his hands in surrender. "About earlier." His face was a picture of regret. "I've been thinking about what you did back there, and I just wanted to let you know I understand.

119

I deserved it. I was rude to Tori, and it was really out of order."

The girls eyed each other suspiciously. *This day is getting weirder and weirder*, thought Alexis. She'd never heard Jordan apologize to anyone, *ever*. Perhaps Tori had gotten through to him after all.

"Tori, I'm *really* sorry I upset you," Jordan continued. He pulled a bag of hard candy from his pocket and gave them to her. "I thought these might help make up for things a bit."

Amber was the first one of the girls to react. "It's a trap, Tori. Don't take them."

Tori hesitated.

"You still don't trust me?" said Jordan, looking hurt. "After I've said sorry and everything." He opened the bag and popped a candy in his mouth. "Look, they're really good, honestly."

"Well . . . he seems genuine enough," whispered Tori to Alexis, still hesitating slightly. She turned toward Jordan. "If you really mean it about being sorry and everything, then I suppose it can't hurt." She reached for a candy and put it in her mouth.

Jordan looked at Adam. They both grinned.

"Nice?" Jordan asked, his pleasant expression replaced with a more familiar leer.

"Ugh!" shrieked Tori, her face twisted in disgust. "It tastes like black pepper — disgusting!" She spat it into her hand.

As far as Alexis was concerned, it was the last straw. "Do you know something, Jordan?" she said. "I've had enough of you and your nasty little stunts. It's about time someone taught you a lesson."

Jordan's eyes flashed at her, and at once Alexis regretted what she'd just said. She felt a flicker of fear she couldn't explain. Without warning, he leaned close. "Alexis," he said, his voice soft as a whisper. "*I am the master at revenge.*" He gave her a knowing smile. "I thought *you* of all people would know that."

At that moment, Miss LaSalle clapped her hands for silence. "When you are *quite* ready, Jordan, the wink murders can begin!"

Alexis hurriedly took her place in the circle, grateful to join Amber and Tori. She still felt shaky from her run-in with Jordan.

"Everyone close their eyes," Miss LaSalle said.

Alexis shut her eyes. The incident with Jordan had

unsettled her, but she couldn't afford to lose her focus now. Not when she'd practiced so hard for this moment. She cleared her mind, trying to block out Jordan's words. The game was all that mattered now, and Alexis prayed not to feel Miss LaSalle's tap on her shoulder. She really, really didn't want to be picked as the murderer or the detective. In the silence, she could make out the ticking of the large chrome clock on the wall.

Miss LaSalle's voice broke the silence. "Everyone, open your eyes."

Alexis breathed a sigh of relief. She hadn't felt a touch on her shoulder. It wasn't going to be her. Beside her, Tori opened her eyes and leaned in to Alexis.

"Look who Miss LaSalle's chosen for detective," she whispered.

Alexis turned to the figure in the middle of the circle. A tall, gangly girl with greasy brown hair and thick glasses stood there, looking as if she wanted the ground to swallow her up.

"Not *Theresa*," Alexis heard Jordan say under his breath. "With her eyesight, we'll all be dead on the floor within a minute. Of all the people to choose! The only one who would have been worse is Tori!"

Alexis looked pointedly at Jordan. "You are *such* a pig."

"That's an insult to pigs!" Amber chimed in.

"Thanks, girls," Tori said, but Alexis could see that Jordan was really beginning to get to her. Alexis squeezed Tori's arm and smiled. She gave her a wink. "Cheer up, girl. He'll get bored with it soon. He is so immature."

"I'll try," said Tori. Then she laughed. "Hey, Alexis, you know what just happened?"

Alexis looked blank.

"You winked at me."

"Did I?" said Alexis in surprise. She hadn't even noticed.

"Just wait until I tell Amber," said Tori. "She'll never believe me."

"It is time for the game to begin," Miss LaSalle continued, with a dramatic arm motion. "Now, we need complete silence. Theresa, good luck, and mystery murderer, good luck. Now begin."

Nothing happened for quite a while, although Alexis couldn't help gripping the sides of her chair in anticipation. *Please let it be me*, she thought, her mind suddenly buzzing with pictures of herself at the theater work-shop being taught by famous actors. Suddenly, Tim Lawton dived off his chair and fell clumsily to the floor. Alexis groaned in dismay. She was going to have to wait for her moment. The first victim of the mystery murderer had been claimed.

Pitiful, thought Alexis. *He could've at least put a little effort into his death.* She could see him peeping and smiling when he was supposed to be a lifeless corpse. But on the bright side, if they were all going to be that use-less, Alexis would have no competition, she would definitely be the best! She glanced sideways at Tori, only to see that she was unusually quiet — and very pale. "Are you all right?" Alexis mouthed.

Tori nodded weakly. "I'm fine."

Alexis wasn't convinced. "Are you sure?" She put her hand on Tori's. It was freezing.

Miss LaSalle stared pointedly at her. "When you've finished, Alexis . . ."

"Sorry, Miss," Alexis said, and returned to the game. She stared at everybody in the circle, hoping to catch the murderer's wink. To her frustration, she saw nothing. Nobody so much as blinked. Across the circle, a sudden coughing broke the silence. Greg Coleman raised a hand to his throat and gave a strangled, choking cry. Alexis watched as Theresa whirled about helplessly, but it was too late. Another victim was dead, and the murderer hadn't been caught.

This time, Alexis was much more impressed. Greg was definitely making an effort; in fact, his death was going on and on and on. He was on his knees, choking and flailing about wildly. It was certainly more entertaining than Tim's pitiful performance.

Alexis fidgeted in her chair. *Why didn't the murderer hurry up and strike again?* She waited, exchanging glances with everyone. But still nobody winked. Alexis didn't have a clue who the murderer was.

She turned to Tori, hoping she might know where the killer was, but her friend was staring steadfastly into the center of the circle, refusing to look around. Alexis reached out a hand and gave her a tap on the leg. Tori's brown eyes glanced momentarily at her before rolling back into her head and then snapping tightly shut.

Not you, too, groaned Alexis inwardly.

But Alexis was stunned at how good Tori's performance was. Of the people who had "died" so far, she was the best by far. Tori had scrambled off her chair and stood hunched over, fighting for breath. Alexis thought that a real asthmatic would have had a hard time competing with this performance. Suddenly, she sank to her knees, clutching at Alexis on the way down, her nails dug harder and harder into Alexis's leg.

"OK, Tori," whispered Alexis. "Stop now — ouch! You're hurting me!" She prized Tori's nails from her thigh and lowered her gently down. As she did so, she noticed her friend's hand felt cold and clammy.

For what seemed like hours, Tori continued to twitch and moan. Fear grew in Alexis as the color began to drain from her friend's skin. She heard the class gasp around her. The whole performance was terrifyingly convincing. Everyone in the class fell silent as their eyes fixed themselves expectantly upon the limp body on the floor. But Tori didn't move.

Someone in the class spoke. "Come on, Tori, stop pretending and get up."

There was no response.

"She's not pretending!" whispered Alexis in a husky voice.

"What did you say?" asked Amber, her voice trembling.

Alexis's voice began to rise. "I said, she's not pretending! Something's wrong." Everyone's faces, including that of Miss LaSalle, seemed stuck in a horrific photograph — no one was moving.

"What are you all waiting for?" Alexis screamed. "Somebody get an ambulance NOW!"

Alexis heard a sob behind her as someone in the class began to cry, but she wasn't worried about anyone except Tori. She dived to the floor and cradled her friend's head. "You're going to be OK, Tori. Just fine." But there was no sign on Tori's face that she understood what Alexis was saying. Hot tears spilled from Alexis's eyes and splashed against the cheek of her unconscious friend.

Suddenly, the entire room seemed to erupt. Miss LaSalle came to her senses, sending Tim Lawton off to phone for an ambulance.

"Tell them it's an emergency!" she shouted after him.

Alexis saw his shocked face disappear down the hallway and prayed for him to hurry. She was dimly aware of Amber chasing after him, anxious to help. All around her the other kids stared quietly in groups, their faces frozen in shock. But Alexis never left her best friend's side.

"Come on, girl," she begged. "Stay with me!"

But as the sound of sirens filled the air, Tori's breath was growing more faint.

Then Alexis felt hands on her arms, lifting her away from Tori. "She will be all right, won't she?" she asked the paramedics. A wave of nausea washed over her as she watched two brightly jacketed ambulance men attempt to resuscitate Tori.

Although she desperately hoped for the best, Alexis knew the truth. Tori's condition was serious.

Very serious.

In the playground, Alexis clung tightly to Amber, her body racked with sobs. All she could think about were the paramedics still inside the studio with Tori. Alexis was so distraught, she barely noticed Amber's tears soaking the sleeve of her sweatshirt.

"This can't be happening," Alexis whispered through her sobs. "I mean . . . she looked a little pale when the game began, but she told me she was fine."

"And I thought the wheezing and stuff were all part of her act," gulped Amber, her cheeks red and blotchy with tears. "If only she'd said something at the beginning — told us she didn't feel well. Then we could've done something earlier."

"I wish I knew what to do," whispered Alexis, tears sliding down her face once again. She closed her eyes, remembering the screams of her classmates as Tori slumped to the floor. Everyone had cried as they'd left the drama studio — even the boys. The only one who'd seemed unruffled was Jordan Franklin. His face was a mask of calm as he passed her in the hallway.

Alexis looked at Amber. "What on earth do we do now?"

But Amber only shook her head, silent tears streaking her face.

Alexis bit her lip hard. She felt so *useless.* Inside the doorway, the two paramedics appeared, talking earnestly with the principal.

"Come on," Alexis said, wiping her eyes and pushing her way through the murmuring crowd. "I want to know what they're saying."

". . . unlikely she'll wake up any time soon," the first paramedic was explaining.

The principal looked grave. "And you don't know how she ended up in this state?"

"Not without further tests, I'm afraid," the paramedic replied.

The principal turned to Miss LaSalle, who was standing nearby. Alexis could see that her skin looked gray, and she was shivering. "I think that under the circumstances, your students should have the rest of the day off." But Alexis didn't want time off. Time off wasn't going to bring Tori back. She wanted to find out exactly what it was that had harmed her friend.

Alexis and Amber wandered home together, trying hard to make sense of it all.

"Why wouldn't they let us stay?" Alexis said sternly. "The police would want to question witnesses, and we were the ones who knew her best." She kicked a crumpled soda can lying on the pavement. "I mean, how can we be of any help at home?"

Amber nodded, looking miserable. "I still can't make sense of it. Tori is the healthiest person I know. I can't even remember the last time she took a sick day."

"That's what I mean," agreed Alexis. "There *has* to be a reason why she suddenly collapsed like that. Whatever caused it must have happened at school!"

"Not necessarily," Amber replied slowly. "I saw a documentary last week called *Mystery Diseases: The Hidden Enemy*. Did you watch it?"

Alexis shook her head.

Amber continued. "Well, according to the program, a rare 'sleeping sickness' has been known to strike victims of all ages. It's caused by viruses lying dormant in the body. People go for years without any symptoms at all, but then one day, something can just trigger the disease and when it does, well . . . there's no telling when they'll wake up."

Alexis shuddered at the thought. She didn't like the idea of Tori having anything horrible like that. "It doesn't seem very likely, Amber. I mean, I've never heard of it."

"It happens," Amber said earnestly. "I think it's one of those mystery diseases that's to blame. After all, if the paramedics don't know what caused it, then what else could it be?"

"I don't know. Maybe it was an allergy or something." But Alexis couldn't think of one thing that Tori was allergic to. Suddenly, her legs buckled, and she had to sit down on the curb in front of a neighbor's house. Her head began to spin, and she fought nausea as her temples throbbed and pounded. Amber managed to get her to walk the last few steps to her own front door.

Alexis's mom opened the door to the two girls and immediately helped Amber get Alexis into a chair.

"Are you OK?" she asked.

"It's Tori!" Alexis said, bursting into uncontrollable sobs. Amber stood by, her eyes trained on the living room carpet.

"Tori? What's happened to her? Is this some kind of joke?"

Alexis threw herself into her mother's arms. "I wish it was. I *really wish* it was."

—

It took until supper for Alexis to feel calmer. Her mom took her by the hand and led her up to her room. "Why did it have to happen to someone like Tori, Mom?" she asked as her mother tucked in the bedcovers.

Mrs. Leigh looked sadly at Alexis and shook her head. "I wish I knew the answer, love, really I do. All I can say is that sometimes, life can be very unfair. We can't always control the things that happen."

"But if I'd acted sooner, Mom, Tori might not be in the hospital."

"You don't *know* that, Alexis," her mom said, stroking her hair. "No one can say that for sure. Tori is obviously a very sick girl. Even a doctor might not have been able to prevent any of this."

But later that night, Alexis was still wide awake. Despite her mother's words, she still searched for answers. All she knew was that Tori was OK before school. There had to be something that happened afterward to change all that. But what?

She listened to her parents talking downstairs in low, worried whispers. Every time her lids grew heavy, images of Tori's frail, lifeless body flooded her mind and haunted her dreams. Alexis buried her head in the pillow, trying to picture a happy and healthy Tori returning to school any day now.

It was the next day, and Amber joined Alexis in the school yard. Her eyes were raw and red-rimmed. They said "Hi" to each other, but neither had the stomach for conversation. Alexis saw Jordan standing in a corner of the playground, with a group of younger kids surrounding him. She felt a knot tighten in her stomach. As she approached, her knot was replaced by disbelief. He was sharing every detail of Tori's collapse.

". . . her eyes were bulging and rolling around in her head . . . and that was when the choking started." Jordan clutched at his throat and began to gag. "Then all this foam and other stuff spewed out of her mouth" — he collapsed onto the bench and began writhing about — "and she was doing all this wriggling and jerking like an electric eel or something."

"Gross," squealed a girl, hiding her face behind her hands. "Did you *actually* see stuff come out of her mouth?"

Jordan sat up. "Oh, yeah. It was like pea soup. Gallons and gallons of it."

Alexis put her hands to her ears, unable to listen anymore. She burst through the crowd, angry tears streaking her cheeks. "You're one sick individual, Jordan Franklin," she said furiously. "Why lie to everyone? You didn't try to save Tori. You hated her. In fact, you're probably glad it happened."

There was an uncomfortable silence before Adam Moran appeared beside Jordan. "Well . . . I suspect she was poisoned."

Jordan shot him an angry look. "Don't be stupid. *Of course* she wasn't poisoned."

"But what about the twitching and stuff?" Adam persisted. "Rats do that when you poison them."

"Adam, just shut up," warned Jordan. "It wasn't poison, OK."

"Oh, and you know better?" Alexis challenged. "Now you're a paramedic, as well as an idiot."

In a second, Jordan had grabbed Alexis by the arm — hard.

"Get off me, you jerk — that hurts!" Alexis fumed.

She could feel Jordan's breath on her cheek as he

whispered in her ear, "I would keep my mouth shut if I were you, Alexis Leigh. You've messed with me before and look where that got you."

"Pig!" spat Alexis, gritting her teeth. "Tori messed with you, too, Jordan, so what did you do to her?"

Suddenly, she felt Amber dragging her away. "Come on, Alexis. He's not worth it."

Alexis rubbed the top of her arm and glared at Jordan. His smile was fleeting, but it was the same one she'd seen on his face when he got back at her for the math test. Her mind recalled how unbothered he had seemed when Tori was collapsing, and suddenly it troubled her. It was almost as if he'd been expecting it. She remembered the argument he'd had with Tori just before drama class. As Amber led Alexis inside, she shot Jordan a backward glance. He was still spouting his gory tale about Tori, and Alexis wondered, not for the first time, exactly what lengths he would go to for revenge.

As you all know, a field trip to the animal shelter was scheduled for this afternoon, and I feel that it would be a very good idea if we still go," Miss Wilson said as all the pupils filed into the classroom. Alexis couldn't bring herself to look at Tori's desk.

Miss Wilson went around the room handing out worksheets, and Alexis realized that she wouldn't mind getting away from school for the day. As soon as the bus driver pulled into the gates of the Safe Haven Animal Farm, her mood lifted a little.

The class got off the bus and assembled by the stables. They were greeted by a prim-faced lady with graying hair. "Hello, everyone," she said. "My name is Celia Ambrose, and it's my duty to welcome you all to the Safe Haven Animal Farm today. And truly, a 'safe haven' is precisely where you are right now. We provide a safe home for the many dogs, cats, and other animals that are unwanted or mistreated by their owners."

Alexis, Amber, and the rest of the class followed Mrs. Ambrose toward one of the barns.

"Now, if you'd like to choose a section to visit, our handlers will be available to answer all of your questions," Celia Ambrose said. "Cats are located along the walkway, dogs in the middle, and rabbits and smaller pets inside the barn at the end."

"I'm going to look at the cats," said Amber. Alexis watched as she wandered off with one of the handlers. Alexis wasn't a big fan of cats. She had always preferred dogs . . . much like Tori. *No — not now*, she said to herself sternly. She tried not to think about Tori. *Tori would have enjoyed it here, so make the best of it.*

She spent some time looking at the chinchillas in the barn, then made her way into the dogs' enclosure. A couple of kennel helpers wrestled with a giant bag of doggie biscuits. There were pedigrees and mongrels, puppies and older, abandoned dogs with graying whiskers. Alexis crouched down in the middle of a shaggy huddle, and immediately a small, scraggy terrier with a white beard tugged at her shoelace and refused to let her pass.

"That's Sonny," said one of the helpers. "He's a real troublemaker. Came to us last year, just skin and bones, red and raw with mange. His owners left him tied up in the yard and barely fed him."

"Come here, you," Alexis said, bending down to stroke him. Tears pricked her eyes as thoughts of Tori flashed through her mind. But just as she was wiping them away a dark shadow fell across the floor. She looked up. It was Jordan Franklin.

"I see you've found a flea-bitten mongrel, Alexis," he said with menace. "And now that I look at you both, I can see you've got a lot in common."

Alexis felt her temper flare, but before she could answer, she heard Sonny begin to snarl. He pulled back his lips and barked angrily at Jordan. Alexis bent down and scooped the dog up in her arms.

Jordan grinned in amusement. "And he's got your nasty temper, too, Alexis. Looks like it's a match made in stray heaven."

"Don't you have someplace better to be?" asked Alexis, struggling to keep calm.

"Not really," said Jordan, smirking. "I just wanted to make sure you found another silly mutt to replace Tori."

Alexis jumped to her feet in fury. If Sonny hadn't got there first, she didn't know what she might have done to Jordan's smug face. But as it was, Sonny jumped from her arms and clamped his teeth around Jordan's right ankle. Jordan yelled in pain and tried shaking the small dog loose, but Sonny hung on grimly.

"Get him off me!" Jordan said, panicking.

A smile crept across Alexis's face. "He doesn't seem to like you very much." She gently tugged at the little terrier's collar. Sonny snarled and then let go.

"If that little idiot had scratched my new sneakers, I would have squashed him," Jordan said to Alexis.

"Well, you know what they say," Alexis replied. "Dogs know who's nice and who's not. It's a sixth sense, apparently."

"That mutt should have a warning label on it," he yelled. "In fact, if you ask me, it'd be better off being put down!"

Alexis looked down at Sonny and, without thinking, winked. She was getting good at winking now, she thought, remembering how impressed Tori had been that day. "Good boy, Sonny," she said, patting his head.

She left Jordan rubbing his ankle, and went off to find Amber before they had to leave.

On the ride home, Alexis watched Jordan limp awkwardly up the steps of the bus before taking his seat next to Adam. Alexis should have been pleased that

Jordan had got bitten by Sonny — it was the least he deserved for his recent behavior — but as she stared at him, he gave her such a smug smile that she felt a tingle of fear.

Alexis sat at the kitchen table, and her mom served her some cheese and crackers. "How was your trip?"

"Great, thanks," Alexis began. "I met this little dog named Sonny. He wouldn't leave me alone. Tori would adore . . ." She trailed off.

"I'm sure she would, honey," her mom said, holding Alexis's hand from across the table. "I'll take you both to see Sonny — as soon as she wakes up."

"What if we adopted him?" Alexis asked suddenly. "He's had such a hard life, Mom. The lady said that Sonny needed someone just like me, who'd give him loads of attention and walk him all the time. His last owners tied him up in their yard and practically starved him."

"Is this a leaflet about the shelter?"

Alexis passed over the brochure.

Alexis's mom looked through it for a moment or two.

"How about after supper, when your dad gets home, we go down there so you can introduce us to this marvelous little dog?"

Alexis could hardly believe it. "Oh, Mom," she gasped. "You won't regret it, I promise."

"I hope not," laughed Mrs. Leigh.

"Mind if I phone Amber and ask her to come?" Alexis asked.

Alexis could hardly believe her ears. "Sick?" she said quietly. "What do you mean, Sonny's sick? I only left him a few hours ago. He was full of life then."

"Why don't you sit down, honey?" Alexis's mom said. "Mrs. Ambrose is going to explain."

Alexis felt numb. She sat down heavily on a chair beside Mrs. Ambrose's cluttered desk. "I can't understand it, that's all."

"Neither can we," replied Mrs. Ambrose. "Poor little guy passed out just after your class left. I've only seen it once before. Starts with terrible wheezing, lungs straining like every breath is torture. The staff called for the vet, but by the time he arrived, Sonny wouldn't wake up." She tapped a pencil against the desk. "It's completely baffling. He's still breathing, but only barely. We're all pretty shaken up, I can tell you."

Alexis was struggling to take this all in. *First Tori and now Sonny!*

Amber put an arm around her shoulders, but Alexis was thinking how Sonny's sickness seemed to be really similar to Tori's. *It has to be a coincidence, right?*

Alexis looked up. "Mrs. Ambrose, you said you've seen it happen once before?"

"Yes. When I was a girl, I lived on my parents' farm. We had a sheepdog who suffered in pretty much the same way. The vet said he had been poisoned."

Alexis sat bolt upright. She felt as though she had been electrocuted. "Poisoned?" she breathed.

"We discovered that some household chemicals had spilled into his drinking water," Mrs. Ambrose said, sadly. "Such a terrible accident."

But Alexis had stopped listening. She had an awful feeling that what had happened to Tori and Sonny was no coincidence . . . and it certainly *wasn't* an accident.

Amber chattered nonstop all the way home. "I hardly think that Sonny's illness has anything to do with Tori," she said. "After all, Mrs. Ambrose told us Sonny showed signs of poisoning. He probably ate something he shouldn't have."

Alexis's mind began to sort through the tangled mess of the memories of the last few days. *Hadn't somebody else suggested poison, too?* She thought back to this morning, and her argument with Jordan in the school playground. Adam Moran had suggested that Tori had been poisoned. But hadn't Jordan immediately dismissed the idea? She rubbed her arm, remembering how he had grabbed at her. And what was it she'd said to him? *Tori messed with you, Jordan, so what did you do to her?*

Mr. Leigh glanced at her in his rearview mirror. "Are you all right, Alexis? You're very quiet."

"Me?" Alexis said, her thoughts crystallizing. "I'm fine."

It was Jordan Franklin.

He had poisoned Tori.

He had also poisoned Sonny.

It all made sense! Jordan had been with Sonny only minutes before the small dog had collapsed, *and* he had had that run-in with Tori on the morning she ended up in the hospital. Alexis felt sick, but at the same time, she felt strangely focused, too. Jordan *hated* being humiliated — surely revenge on Tori and Sonny was the perfect motive!

Alexis tried organizing the series of events leading to Tori's collapse. Only minutes before the game of Wink Murder had begun, Jordan had offered Tori some candy, and she became sick just after that. Jordan must have done something to the candy that he offered Tori, and popped an ordinary piece into his own mouth as cover.

Alexis was sure that she hadn't seen Jordan give Sonny anything to eat . . . but she *had* left them alone together as she went to get on the bus. It couldn't have been that long, but Alexis was sure it was long enough for Jordan to have slipped the dog something harmful.

He *had* taken revenge on both of them . . . and he had done it with poison! All Alexis had to do was find out how.

The janitor had barely hung up his coat in the staff-room when Alexis arrived in school. She crept down the hallway toward her homeroom. Peeking through a crack in the door, she could see that there was nobody in yet — not even Miss Wilson.

Alexis hesitated in front of Jordan's desk. Under normal circumstances, it would never have entered Alexis's head to be rifling through someone else's private possessions. She tried not to think about what might happen if she were caught and prepared herself for what she had to do. *These aren't normal circumstances,* she told herself, *and Jordan Franklin is* definitely *not a normal boy.*

At first glance, there appeared to be nothing strange. A few assorted books with pictures doodled on the cover, textbooks, three tooth-marked pencils, and a half-eaten apple wearing a moldy overcoat. *Maybe there's something underneath,* Alexis thought. As carefully as she could, she rummaged deeper, but to her disappointment found nothing. Absolutely nothing. Alexis felt desperate. *This can't be right,* she thought. *There has to be something.*

"Alexis Leigh! What are you doing inside Jordan's desk?" demanded a voice from the doorway. Alexis felt as though her heart would explode through her chest. It was Miss Wilson, her homeroom teacher.

"Um . . . er . . ." said Alexis, panicking. She could feel her cheeks burning. She looked in desperation at the clutter inside Jordan's desk. Her eyes fell on a scruffy-looking book with doodles of test tubes on the cover.

Quick as a flash, Alexis picked up the book and waved it at Miss Wilson. "Chemistry book, Miss Wilson," she said. "Jordan said I could borrow it to copy some notes."

Alexis felt her skin prickle. *That had to be it! Chemistry! There are plenty of poisonous things in a chemistry lab.*

Miss Wilson looked at her for a moment longer. "Hmm — well, just this once, I suppose. You know the rules, Alexis," she said, dropping an armful of books on her own desk at the front of the class. "Now go outside until the bell rings, please."

Instead of going outside, Alexis headed for the library. It was double chemistry that morning, and Alexis was determined to research poisons before she got there. She kept thinking about Jordan's expression at the animal shelter. It reminded her of the way he'd looked at Tori that fateful morning. A chill ran down her spine.

Alexis frantically scoured the Internet for clues. She had to find out what poisons Jordan might have taken from the science lab. She glanced anxiously up at the clock. There were only a few minutes until homeroom, and then chemistry.

She hit the search engine button for what felt like the hundredth time, and suddenly something was there, right in front of her on the screen. A chill ran down her spine, an icy hand gripping the back of her neck.

ACHERONIA CHLORIDE: If taken internally causes constriction of the airways, convulsions, and fainting. If taken in large enough quantities, may induce coma. This can be found in factories and laboratories.

Acheronia chloride . . .

Alexis was *sure* she'd seen it in the school chemistry lab. The lesson bell sounded, and she made her way to the classroom, slipping Jordan's book back into his desk before anyone else arrived. Alexis's heart thumped against her chest as she considered her options. She could wait for Jordan to make a move, and catch him stealing poison. But that left too much room for error. What if Jordan didn't try anything this week? How would she actually prove it? It would be like the mouse incident all over again. No proof. She tried not to think about what might happen then. No, there *had* to be another way. She had to remove the poison altogether.

The class filed into the chemistry lab, and Alexis took her regular seat. To her frustration, she found Amber leaning across the Bunsen burners, arguing with Jordan. He was smirking, with Adam Moran at his side.

Alexis saw Amber point at Jordan. "You need a license to bring toxic waste like you into school."

Jordan's face clouded. "You ought to watch that mouth of yours, Amber," he said. "It's going to get you in serious trouble."

At that moment, Mr. Malone, the chemistry teacher, entered the room.

"OK, everybody," he said, shrugging on a well-worn lab coat. "I need somebody to help me distribute the chemicals for today's experiments."

It was just the opportunity Alexis needed, and before he could finish buttoning his lab coat, she was at his side. "I'll help, Mr. Malone," she said.

He accompanied her to the rear of the room, where a locked cabinet contained all of the dangerous chemicals. "We'll be studying oxidization today," he said with a jangle of keys, "so we'll need a lot of nails."

Alexis's eyes scanned the shelves. There it was! Acheronia chloride. It was on the third shelf, beside the plastic container of iron nails. For a second, she considered stealing it. She only had to slip it in her pocket, and it would be out of Jordan's reach. But what would she do afterward with a bottle of poison? It might harm the water supply if she poured it down a sink, or she might end up getting caught. And then another solution popped into her head — the only permanent solution Alexis could think of. She reached across and grabbed the plastic container full of nails, making sure she gave the bottle of poison a sharp knock at the same time. It flew across the shelf and smashed to pieces on the tiled floor.

Mr. Malone threw his hands up in fury. "That was

the only bottle of acheronia chloride we had, and it's very expensive to replace! Honestly, Alexis, I thought you could be trusted."

"Sorry," Alexis replied. "I'll help you clean it up." But she wasn't sorry! She felt enormous relief.

"No, you will *not* clean this up," Mr. Malone said. "This stuff is poisonous. You'll have to find the janitor. He'll know how to dispose of it safely."

Smiling to herself, Alexis headed for the door. On the way, she couldn't help but shoot Jordan a triumphant glare. Oddly, Jordan appeared completely unconcerned about the whole incident. He was more interested in trying to light the end of his pencil with a Bunsen burner. Alexis could feel a frown clouding her face. *Shouldn't Jordan be furious with her?* She'd just destroyed his poison, and he didn't seem bothered at all.

She proceeded to the janitor's office feeling more and more confused. For the first time, she began to seriously doubt what she had believed about the poison. Maybe Jordan hadn't poisoned Tori and Sonny after all. Maybe he'd used another method. Or, even worse, maybe he'd had nothing to do with any of it.

She went over and over the events of the last couple of days as she walked down the hallway. It *had* to be Jordan. After all, who else had had the opportunity to do it? Apart from him, there had only been Alexis herself who'd been with them before they'd collapsed.

She knocked on the janitor's door and explained what had happened. He gathered his mops and buckets and departed for the chemistry lab.

All of a sudden, Alexis felt worn out. The tragic series of events must have affected her more than she knew. She was exhausted, and it was only the first class of the day. On her way back to the lab, she stopped by the girls' room so that she could get ahold of herself.

She splashed cold water on her face and tied her hair back into a ponytail. *Well*, she said to herself, *you've done everything you can.* Things now seemed a million miles away from the normality of the week before. She inspected her hair in the mirror over the sink — and winked at her reflection. Alexis was getting good at it now. And then she stopped and stared at herself again.

A wink.

That's how the whole thing had started! With a

dumb old game of Wink Murder. The game, the drama lesson — it was all so meaningless now, yet it had seemed so important at the time.

Her footsteps echoed in the hallway as she hurried toward the chemistry lab. But since leaving the girls' room, Alexis's chest felt tight, and her breathing had become labored. Perhaps it was the anxiety of what had happened, or it could even be her imagination, she reasoned to herself as she walked on.

But it was getting worse.

Alexis was struggling for air, and she began to feel incredibly lightheaded. She could actually *feel* her eyes rolling back into her head. In terror, she desperately reached for the door handle to the chemistry lab, but instead, her legs crumpled beneath her. It felt as though a large weight had been dropped on her, pressing her to the floor. She began to feel her body jerk and writhe. There was nothing she could do to stop it.

It was at that moment that Alexis realized the terrible truth about who had *really* caused Sonny to play dead. And Tori, too.

It wasn't Jordan Franklin.

It was Alexis.

As Alexis's breathing slowed to a dull murmur, snapshots flooded her brain. She pictured herself giving her best friend Tori a friendly wink in drama class just before the game had started. She also winked at Sonny for biting Jordan's ankle. Finally, as a strange trance stole any remaining energy, Alexis recalled winking at her own reflection.

Too late, Amber's words came back to haunt her: *"If you remember what I've told you, Alexis, you'll soon be able to give the perfect killer wink. . . ."*